MW00561457

Waila
on the
Hiking
Trail

Written & Illustrated by Jessica Paige Dawson

Have you ever heard the tale of Waila on the hiking trail?
They say it's just a fairytale, a myth, or nursery rhyme.

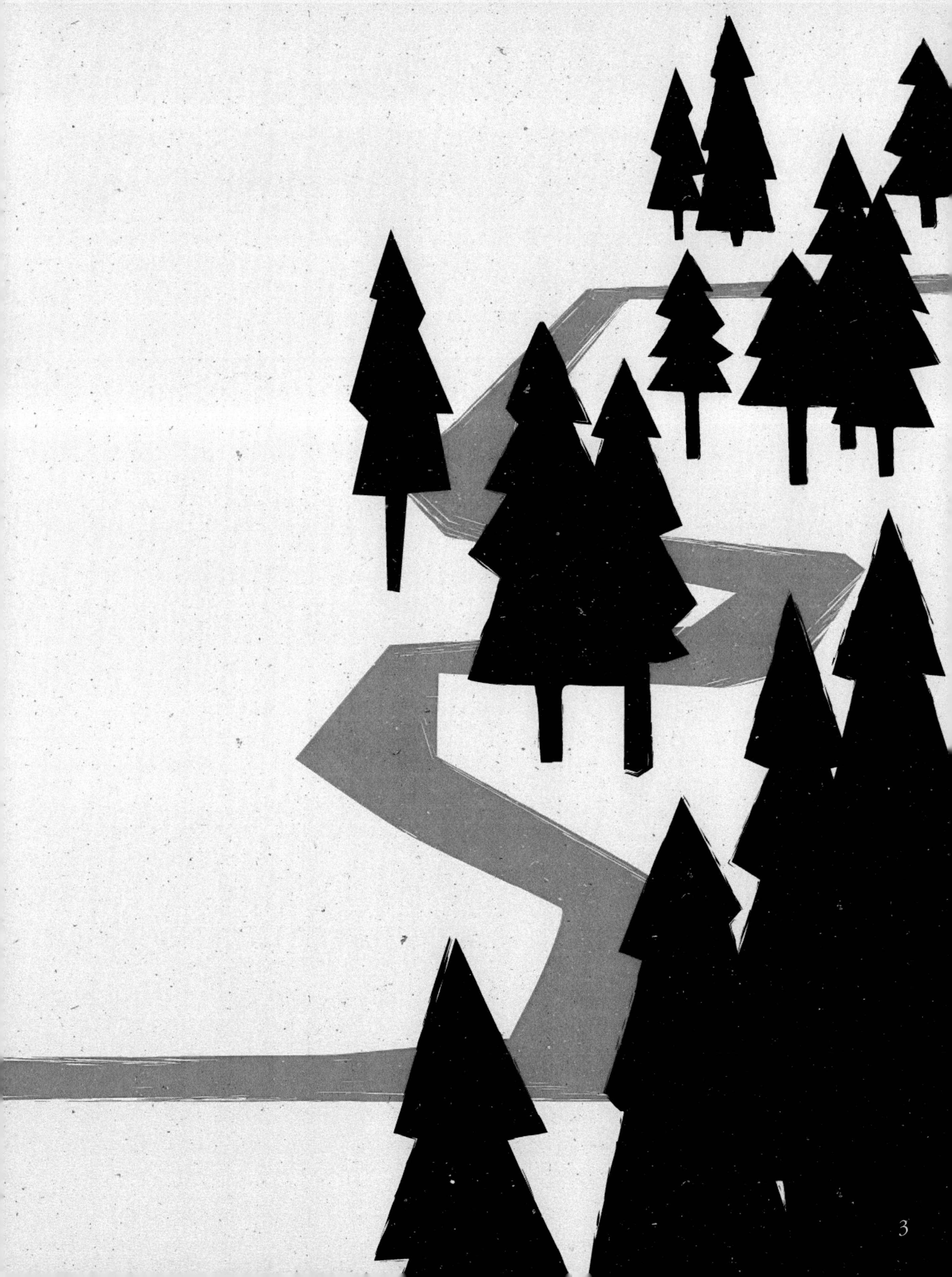

It happened not so far from here, where hikers gathered every year.

They marched with sticks and packs of gear, their boots all caked with grime.

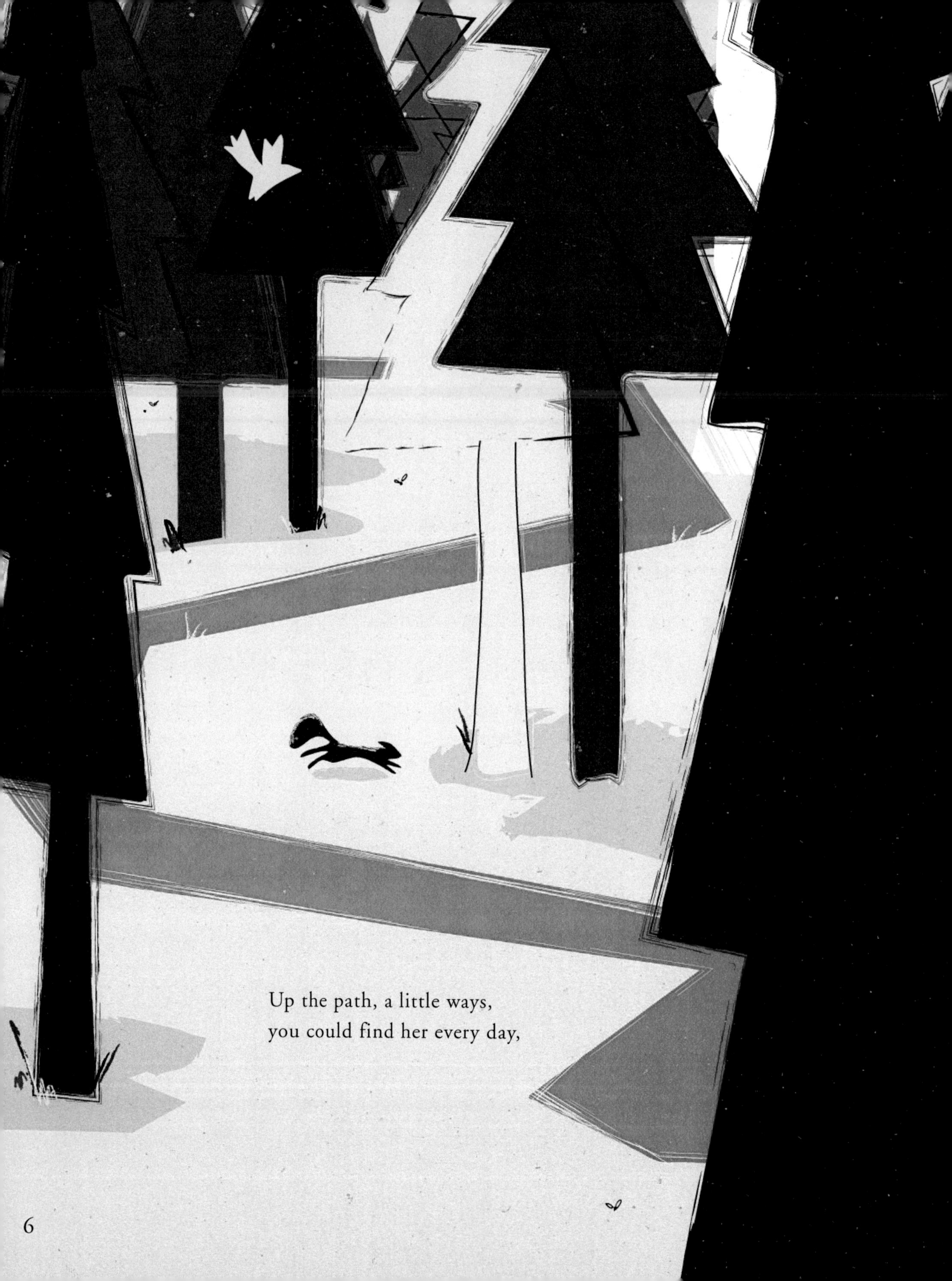

Up the path, a little ways,
you could find her every day,

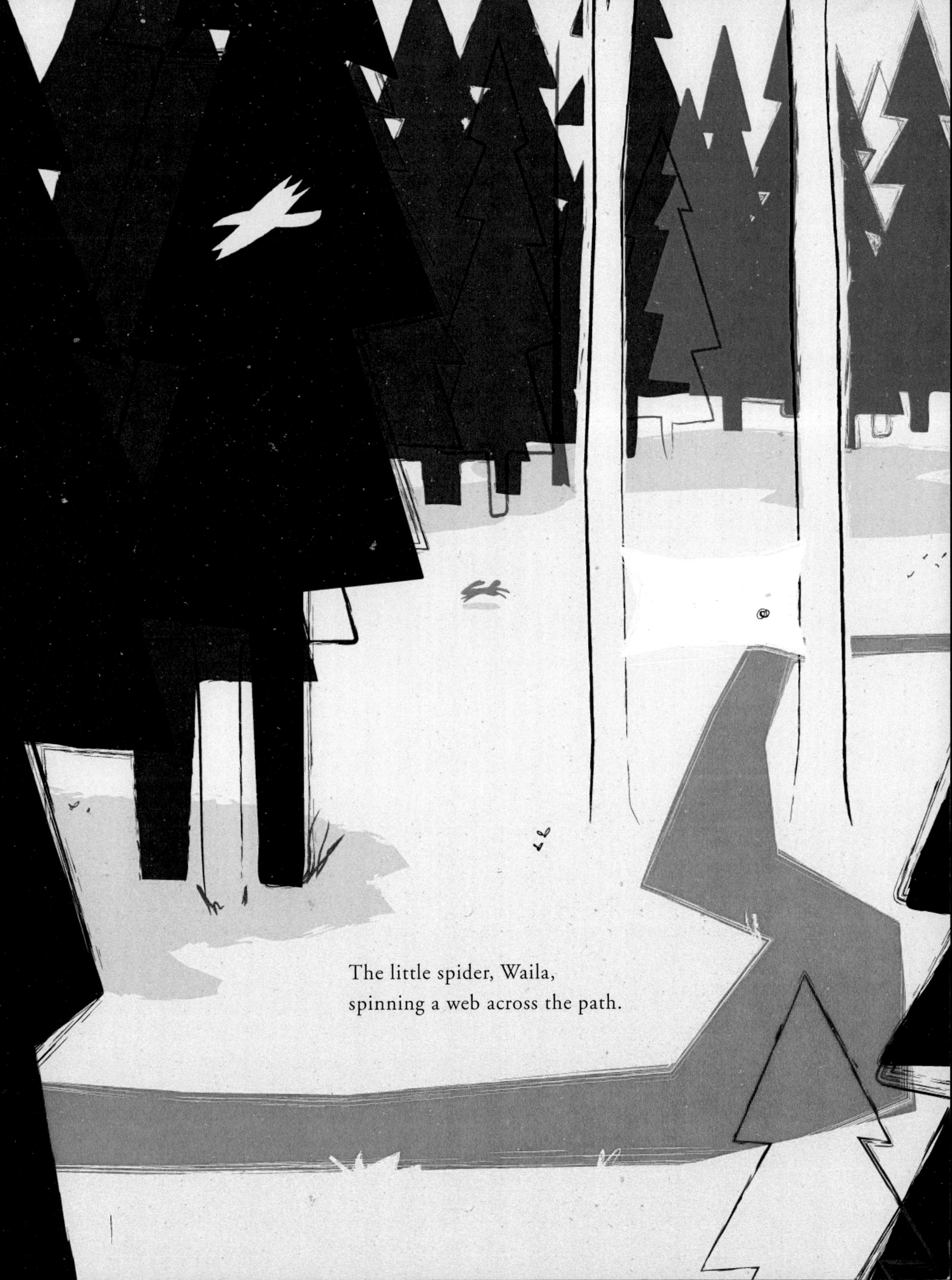

The little spider, Waila,
spinning a web across the path.

Of course, her web would not last long.
Not because it wasn't strong,
but whenever hikers came along ...

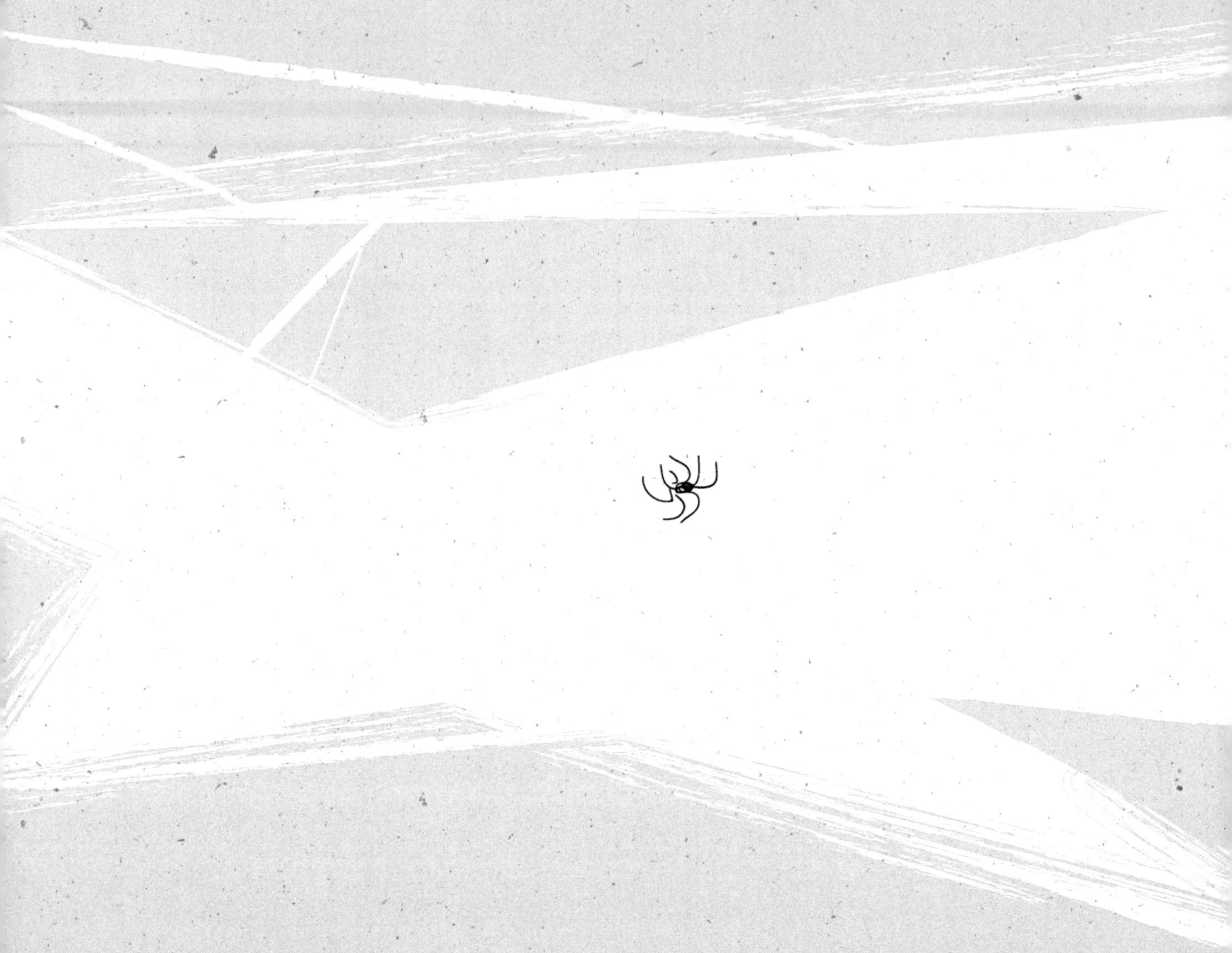

they stomped through it as they passed.

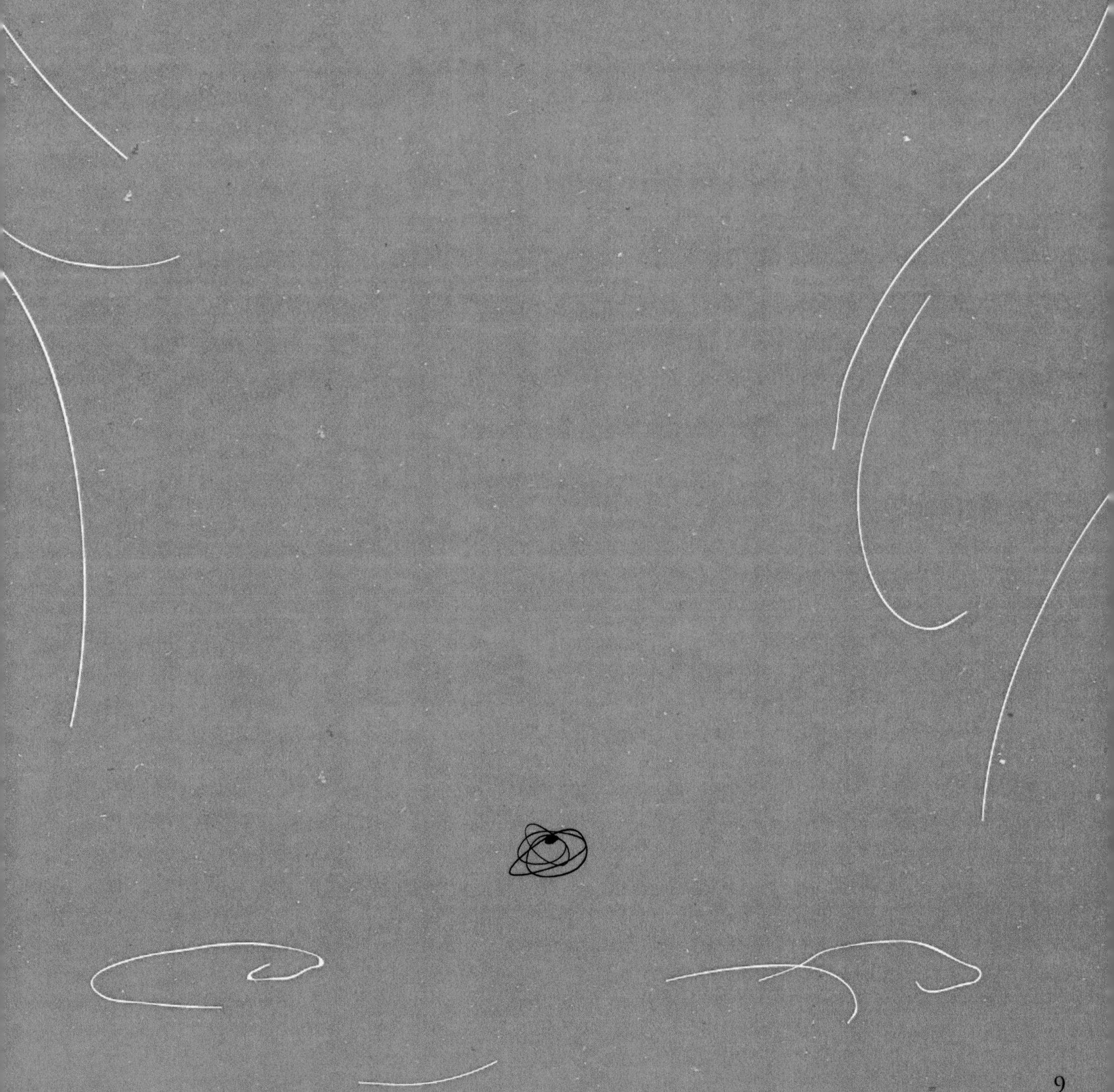

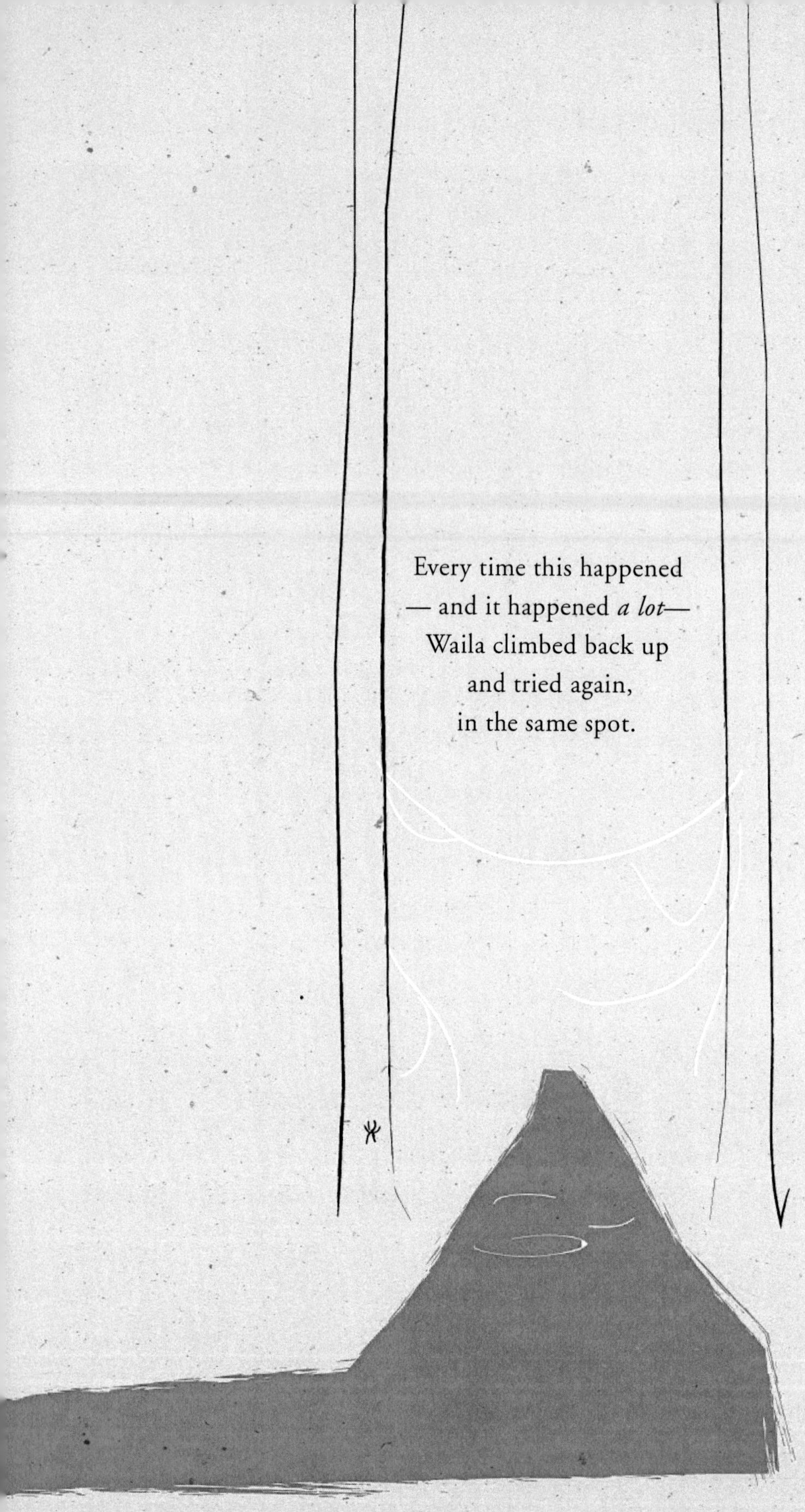

Every time this happened
— and it happened *a lot*—
Waila climbed back up
and tried again,
in the same spot.

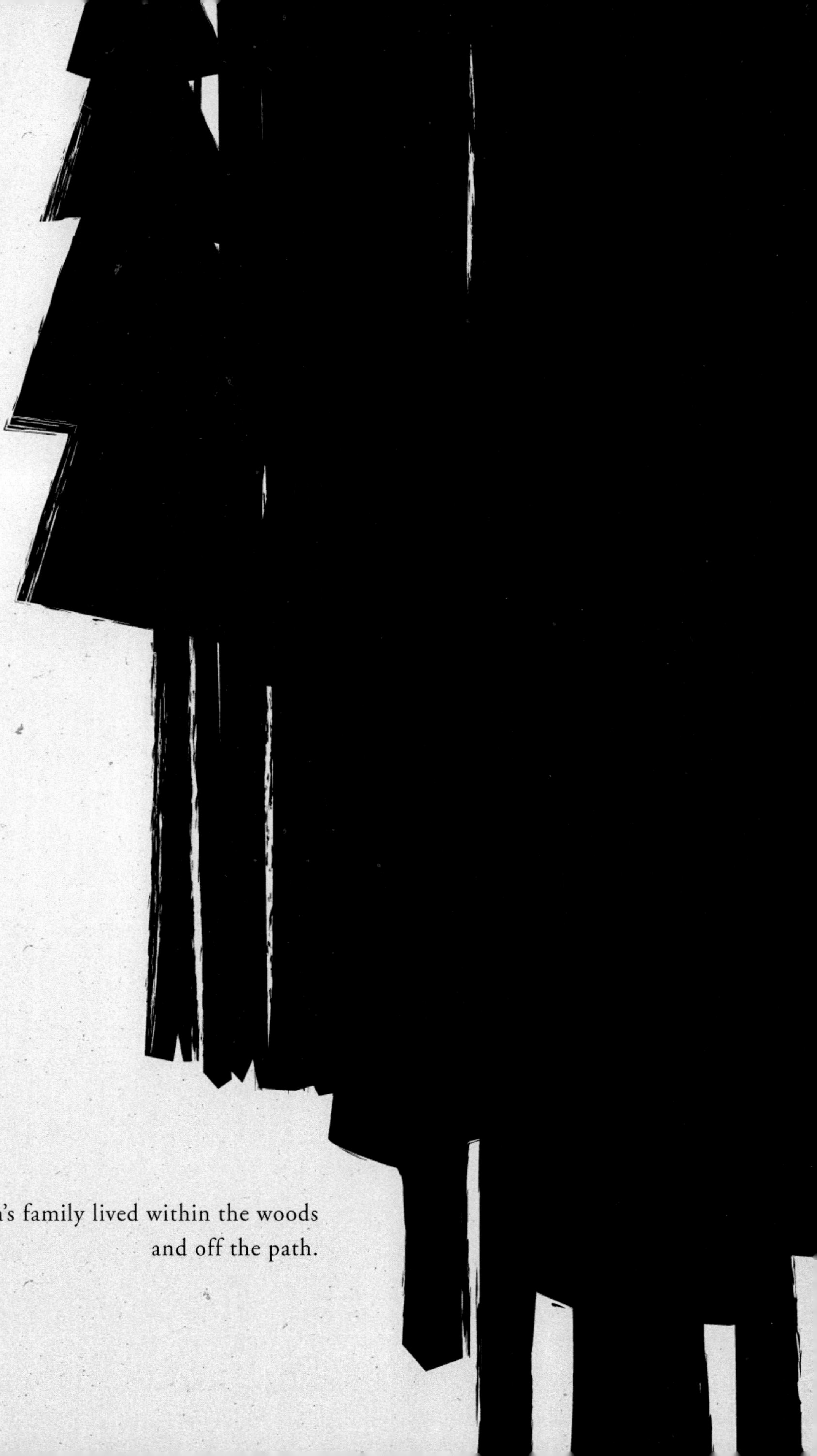

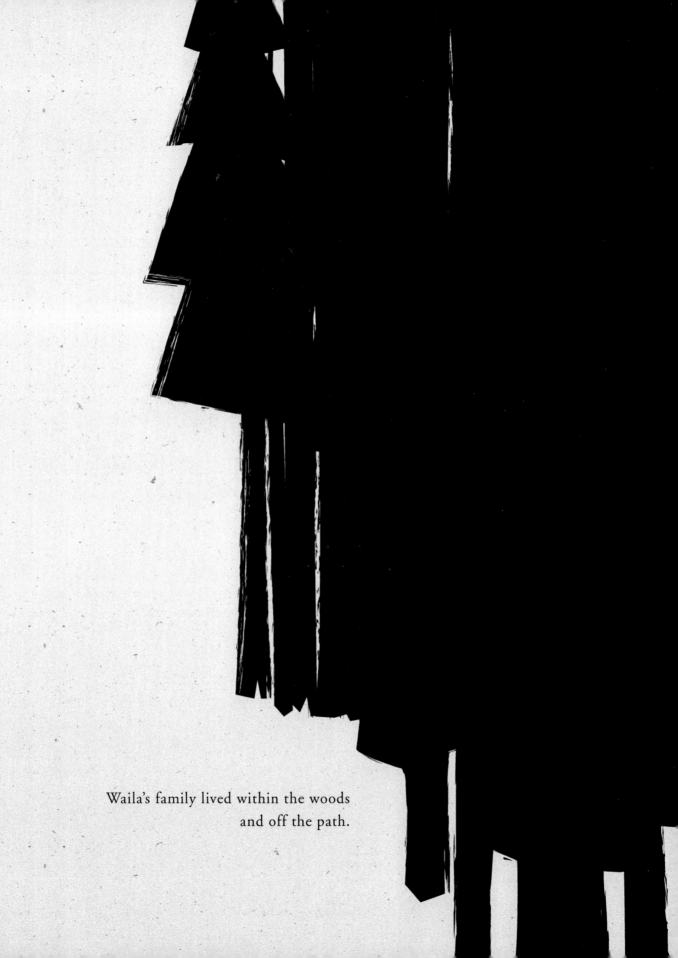

Waila's family lived within the woods
and off the path.

Hikers never found them,
so their webs would last and last.

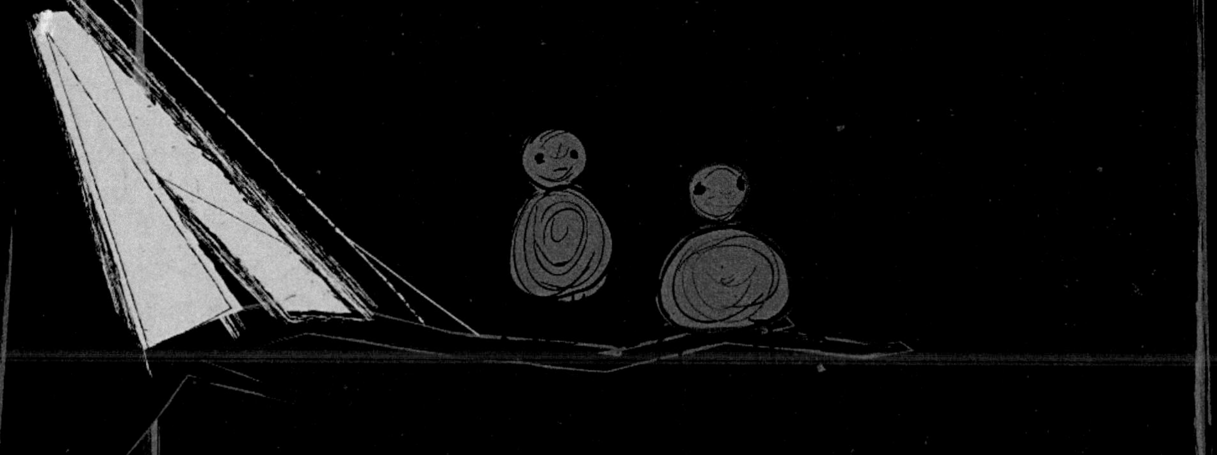

Because they didn't spend their days
repairing webs the hikers thrashed,

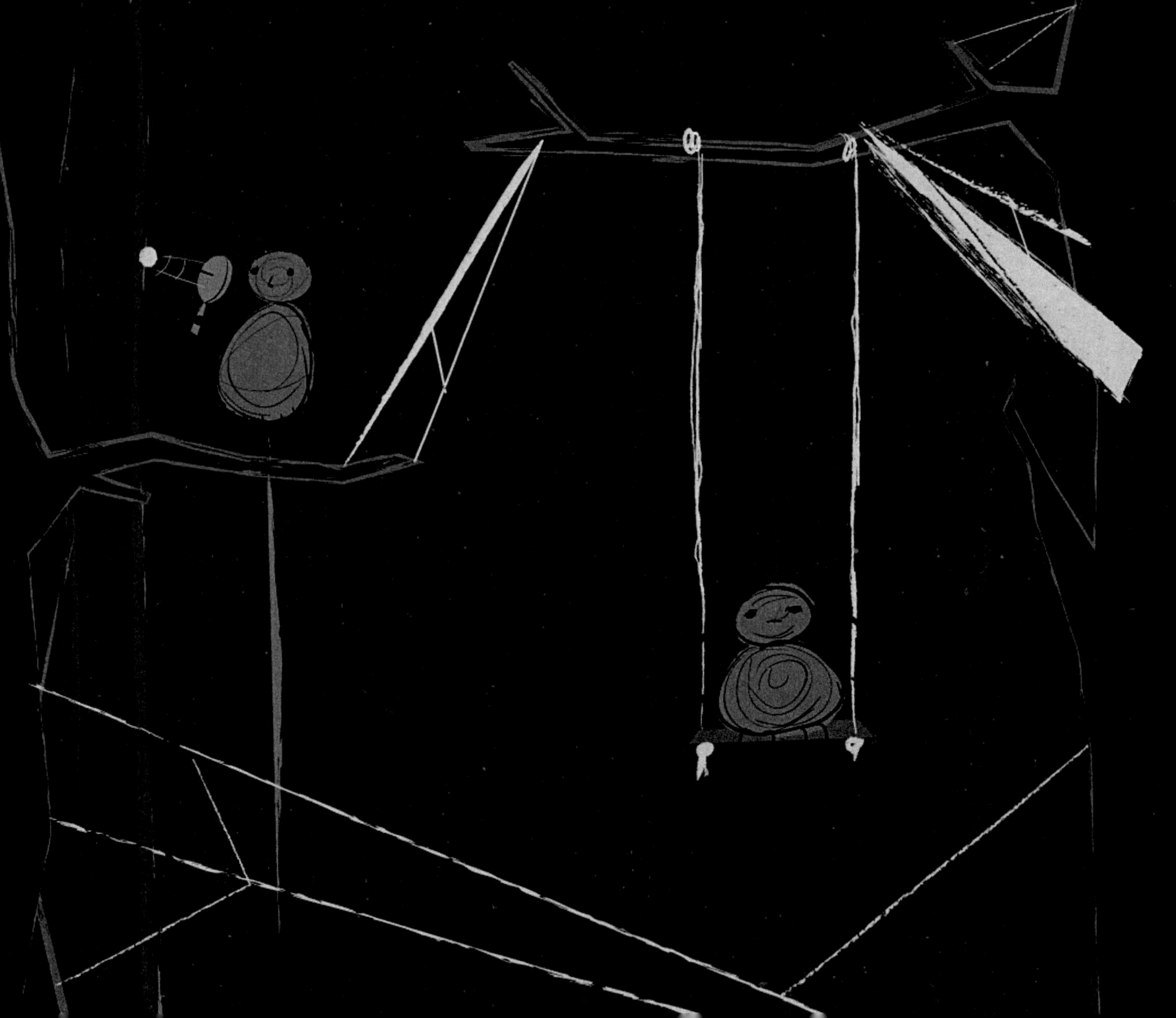

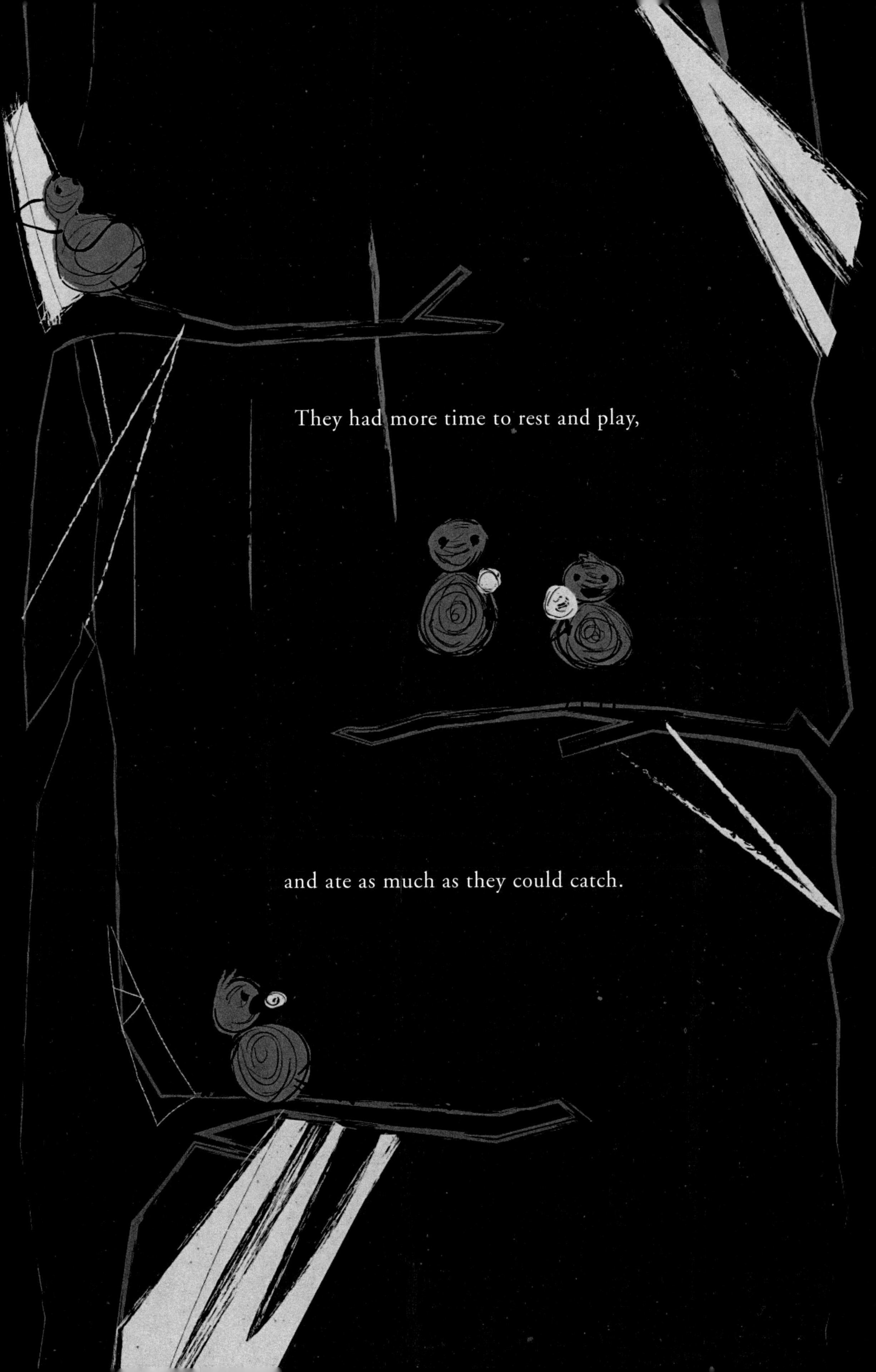

They had more time to rest and play,

and ate as much as they could catch.

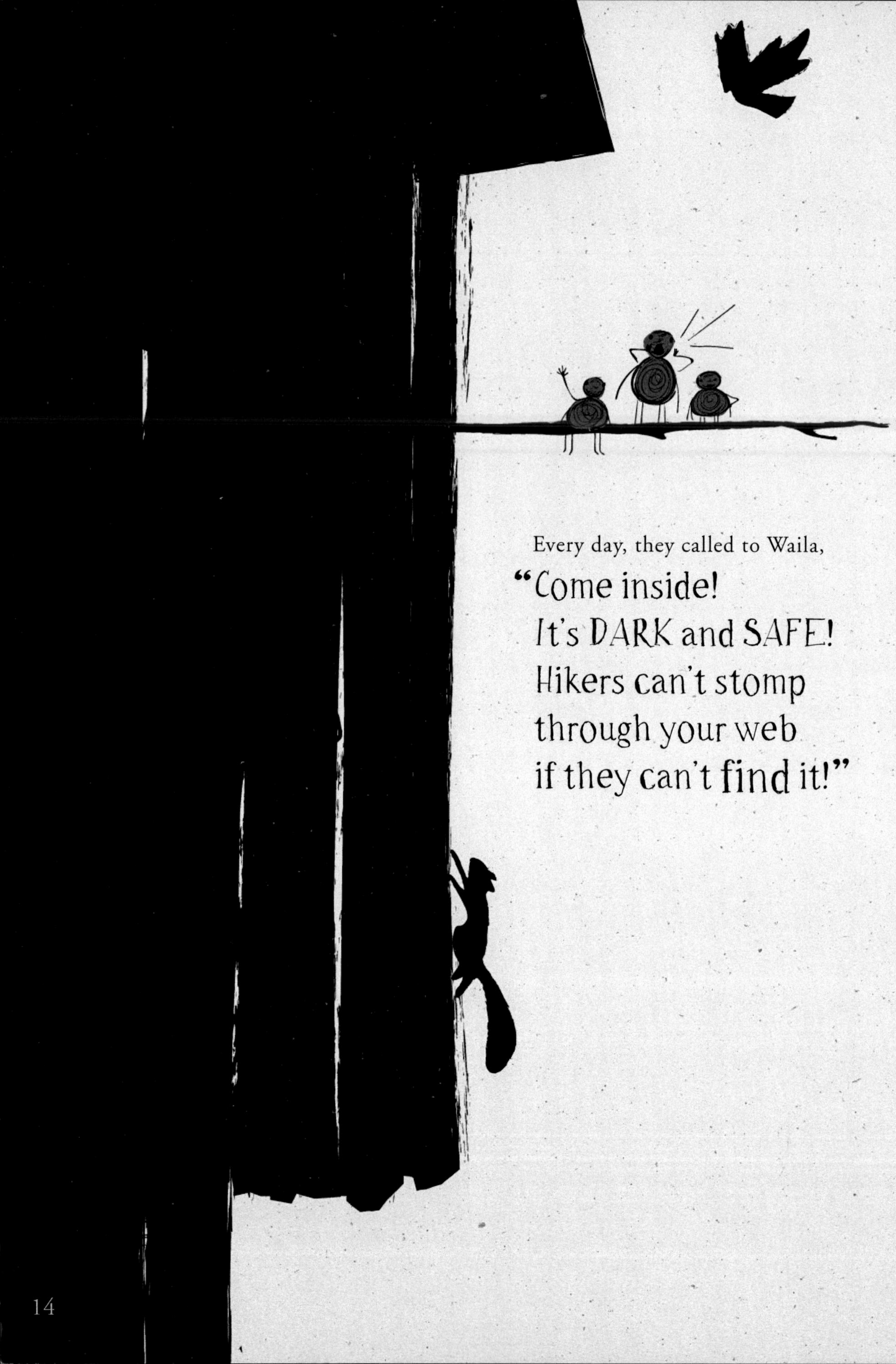

Every day, they called to Waila,

"Come inside!
It's DARK and SAFE!
Hikers can't stomp
through your web
if they can't find it!"

Waila stayed.

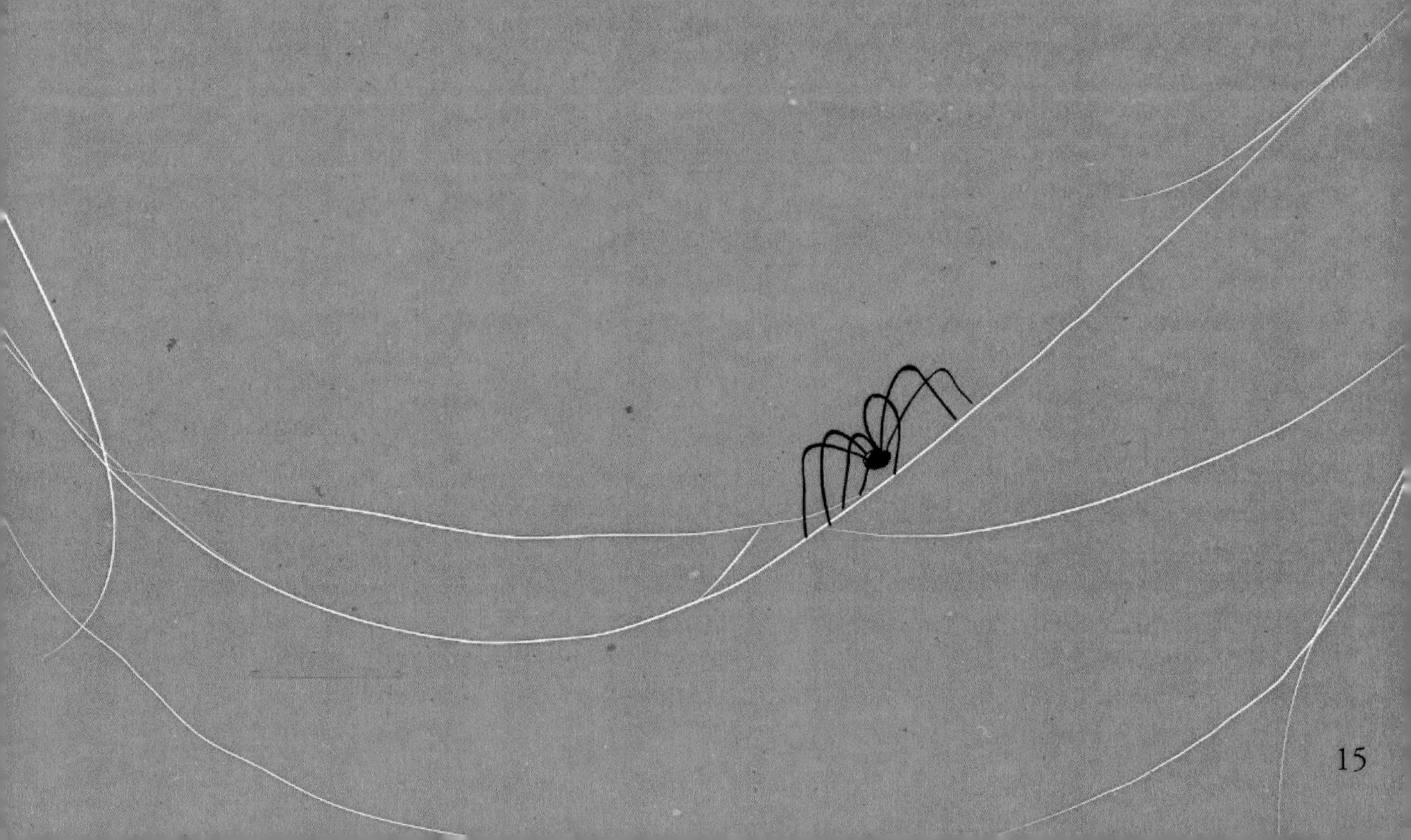

At night, the trail was closed and all the woods was calm and dreamy.
While all the spiders dozed off, only Waila stayed up weaving.

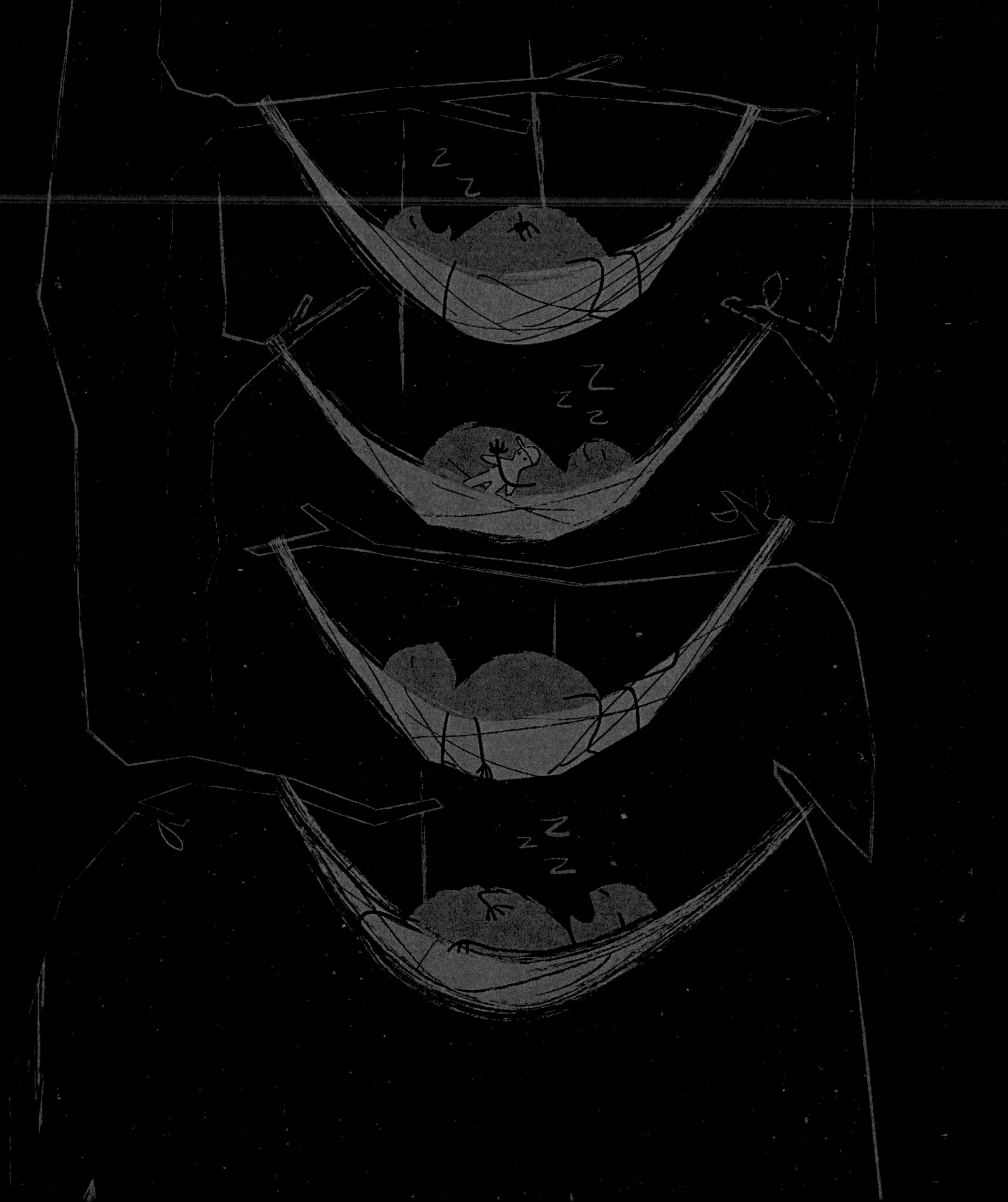

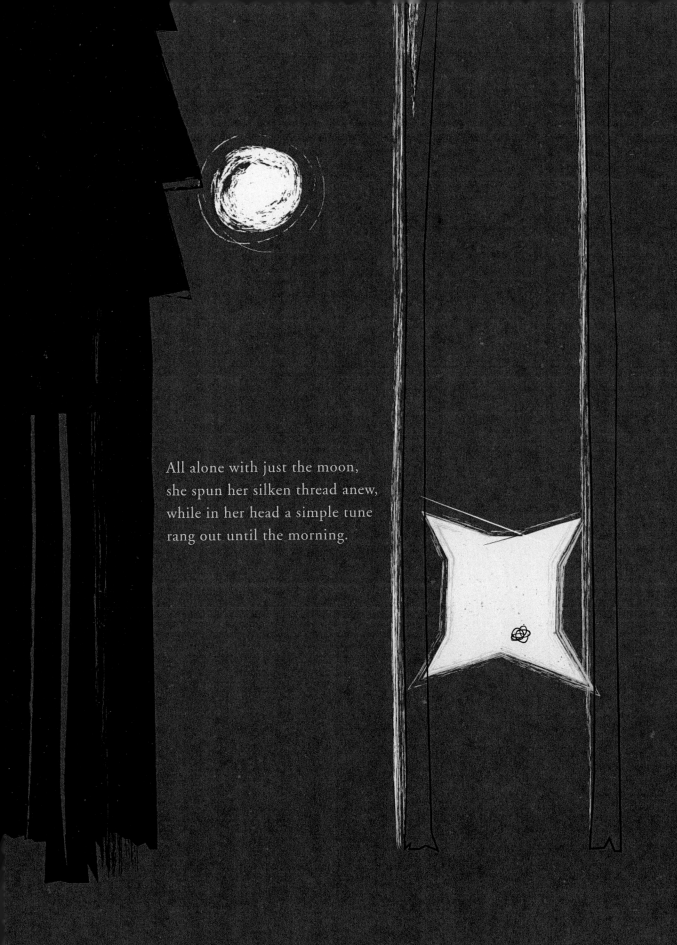

All alone with just the moon,
she spun her silken thread anew,
while in her head a simple tune
rang out until the morning.

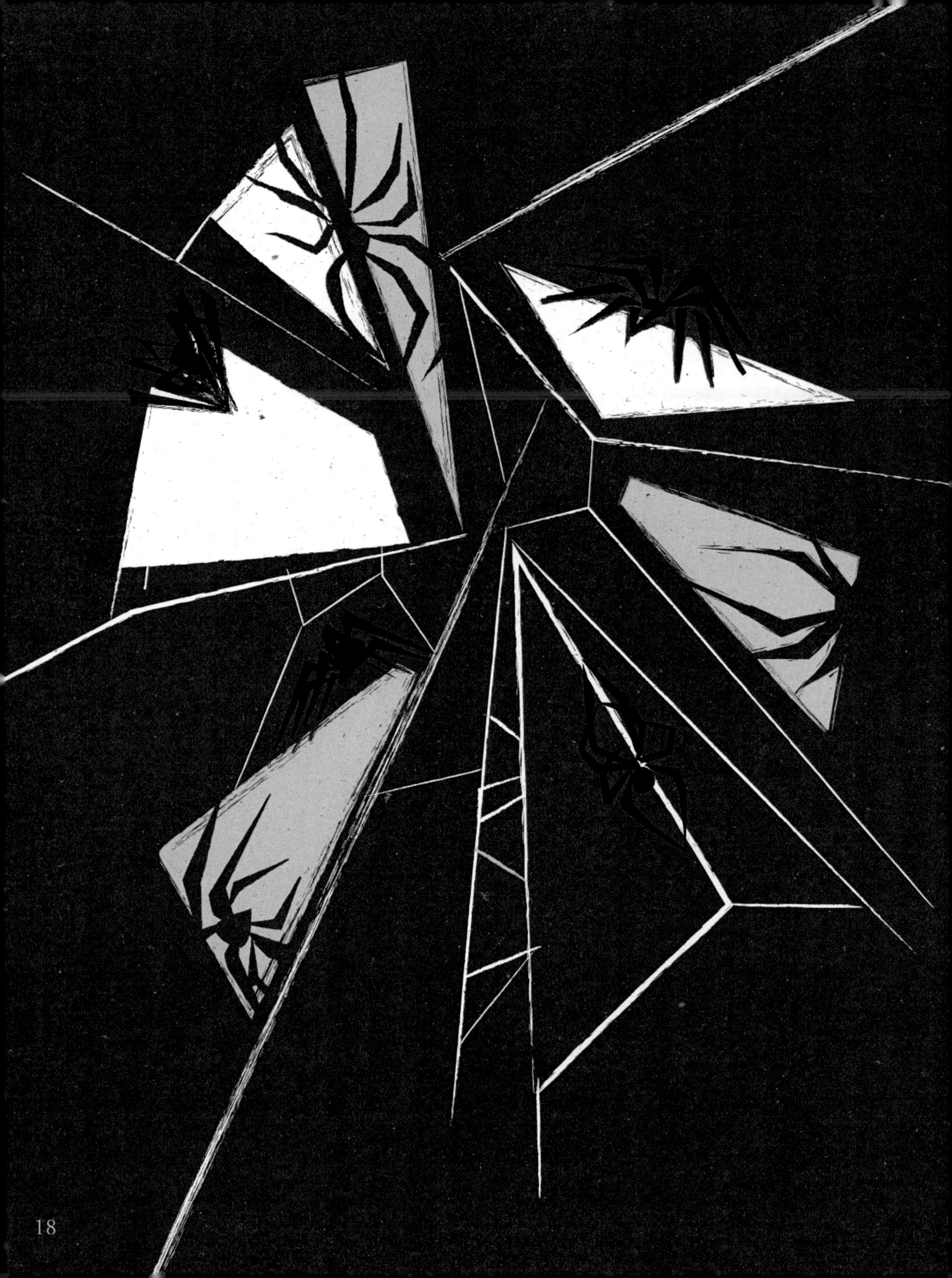

Weaving, weaving, sleep — repeat.
Her eight legs thread on tirelessly.
Spinning faster, twining, winding,
Binding thread in record timing.

Dipping, wrapping, pulling taut,
Her work would shame a sailor's knot.
Through each web the hiker's tread,
Her thread is torn,
her will is not.

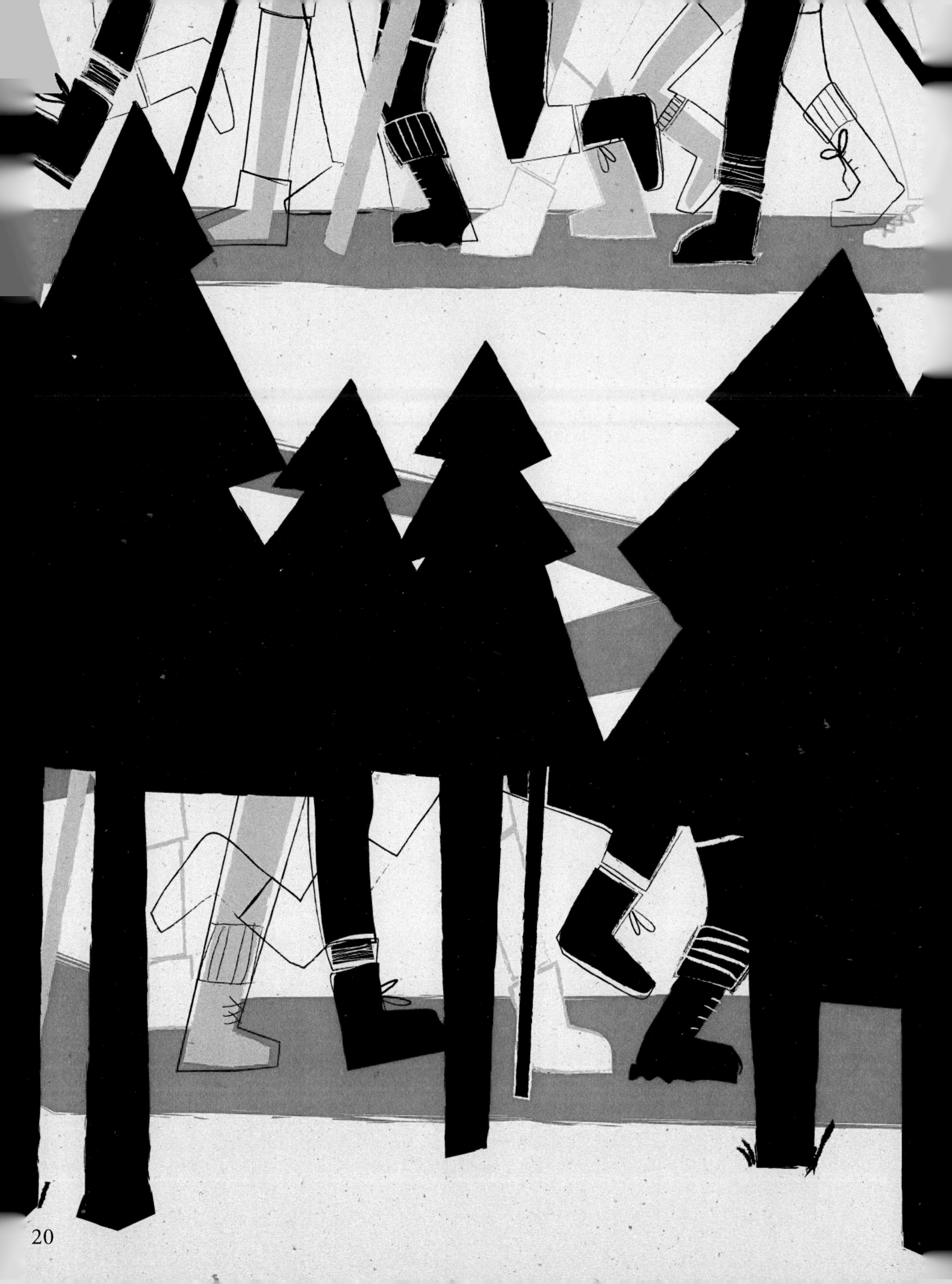

With the morning came more hikers stomping up the path.
All the woodland creatures scattered, only one stood fast.

Waila's web, all fresh and
new, and gleaming with
the morning dew —

was all-in-one-go

trampled through

by the day's first hiker.

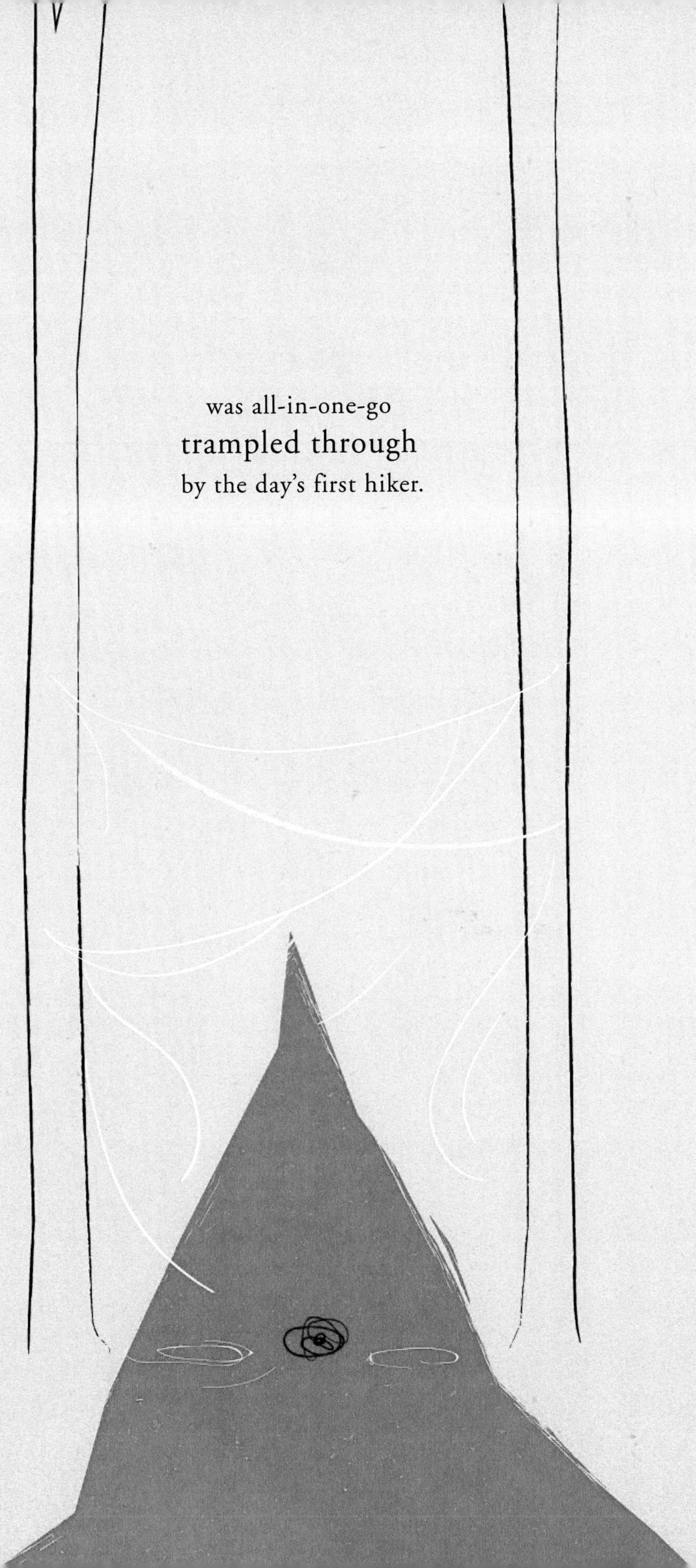

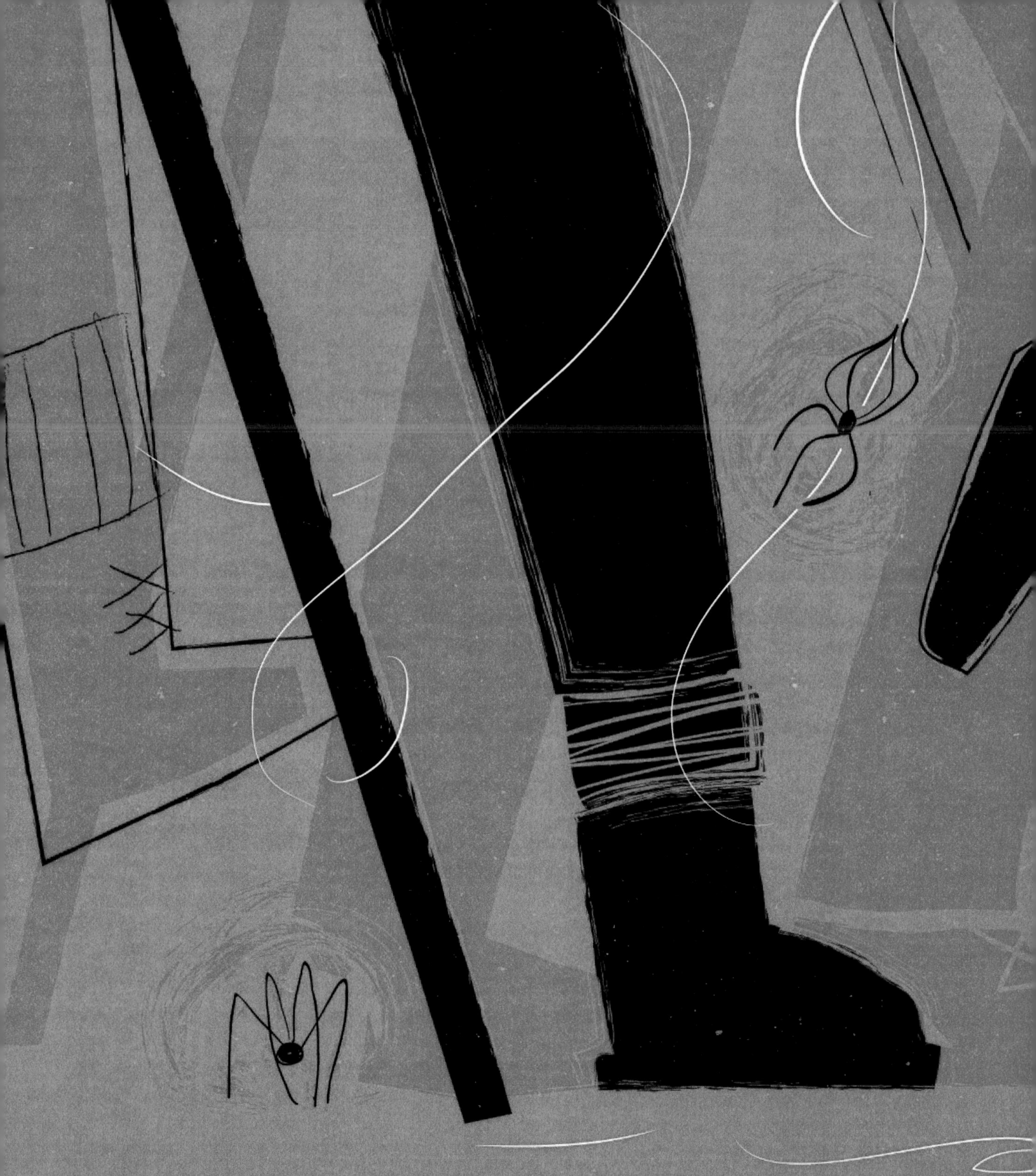

After that, the flood gates parted! In they poured at a constant pace!

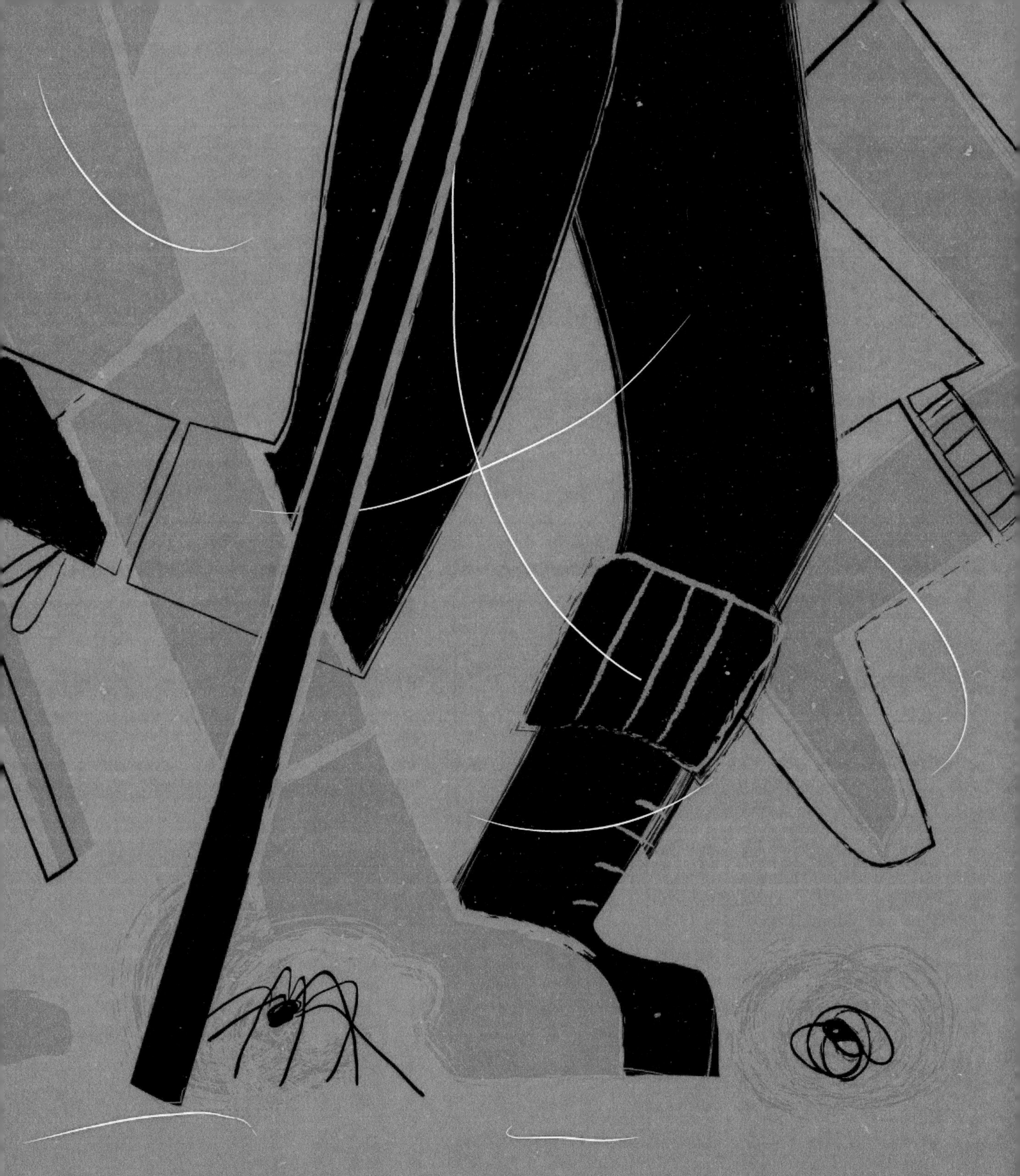

Each new web that Waila started met the same sad, gruesome fate.

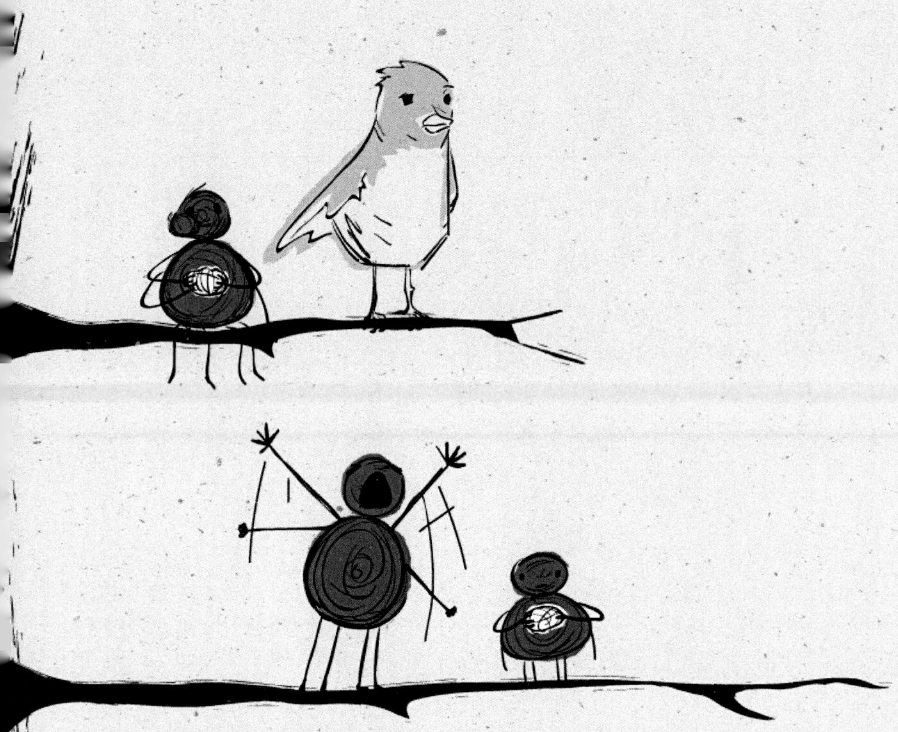

Cried her family from a distance,

"Waila, quit this silly business!
Your web is SHREDDED!
This path is pointless!
It's time to STOP this!"

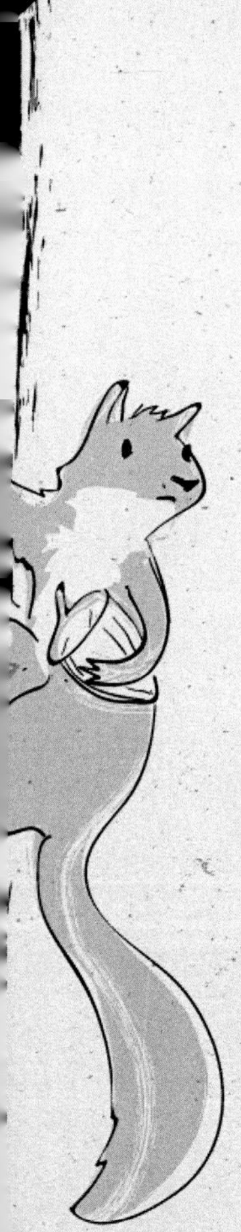

Waila persisted.

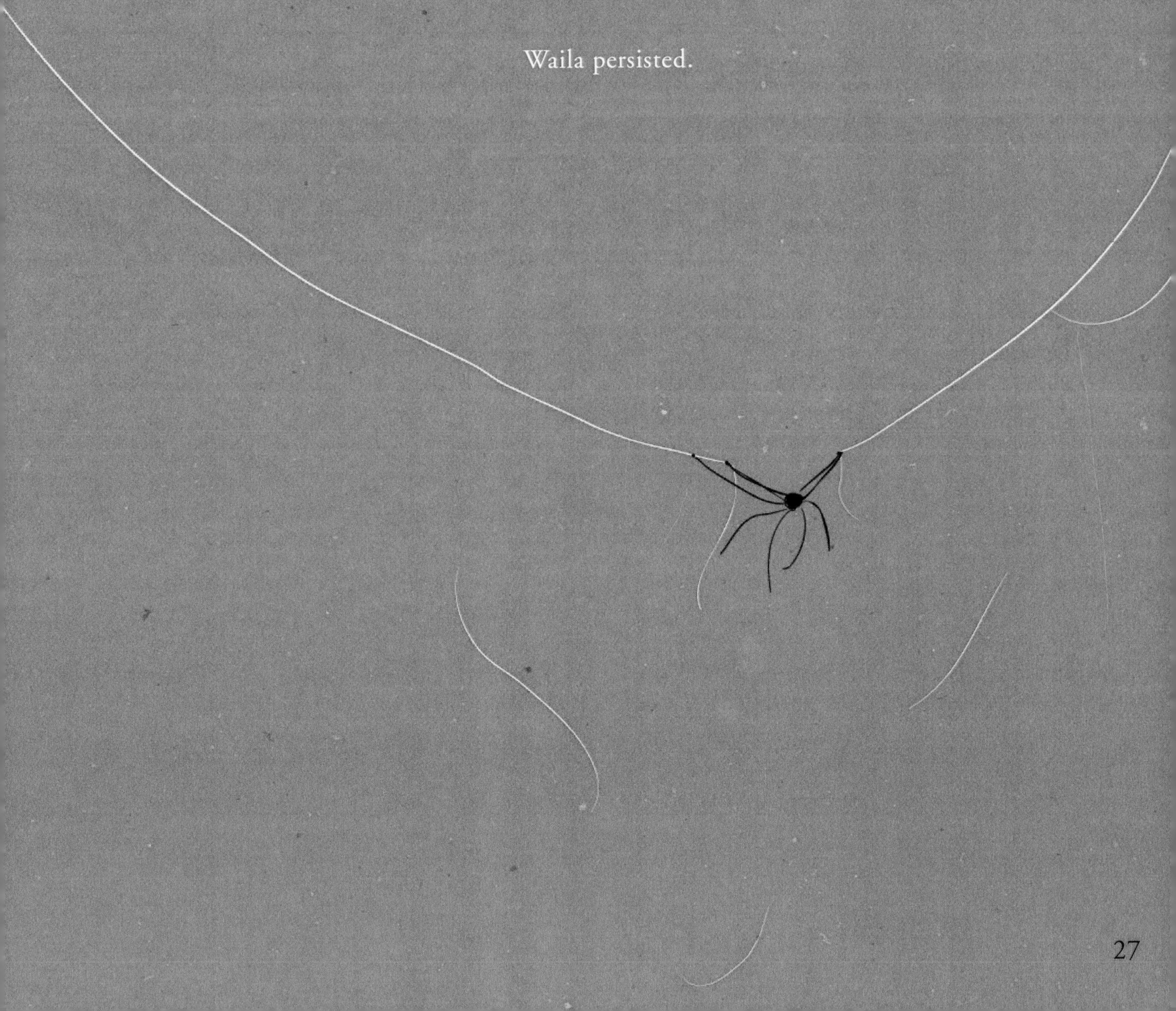

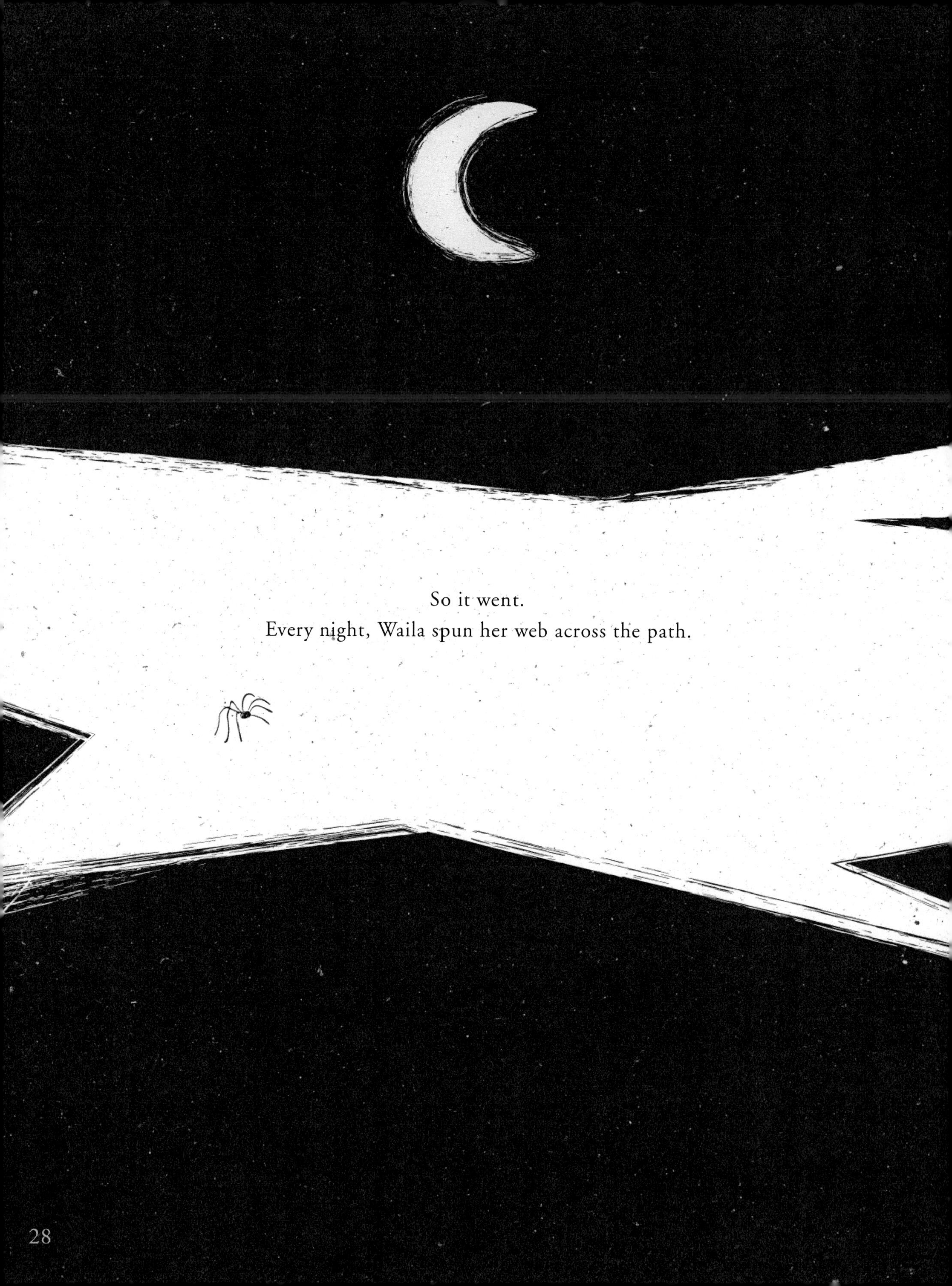

So it went.
Every night, Waila spun her web across the path.

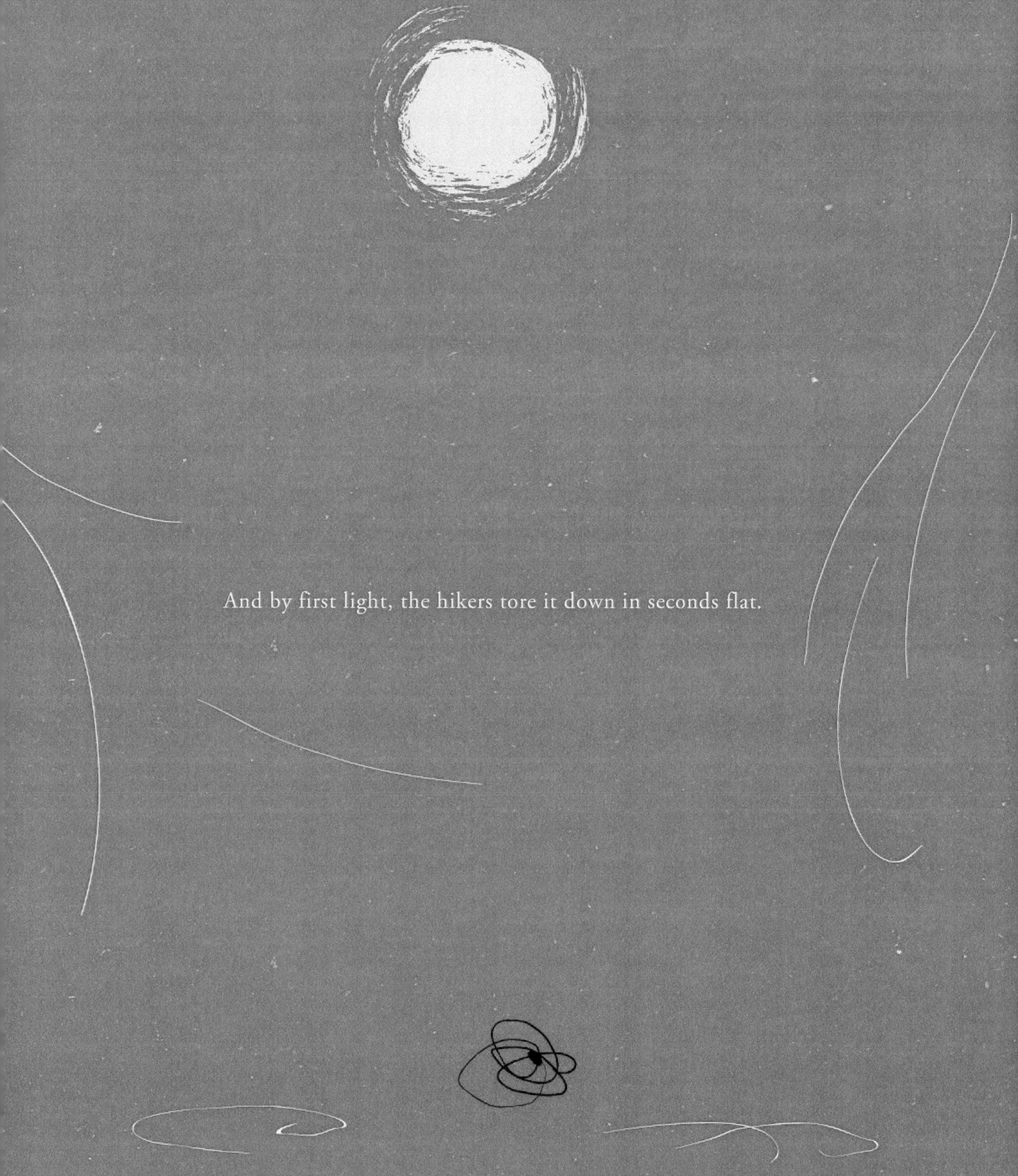

And by first light, the hikers tore it down in seconds flat.

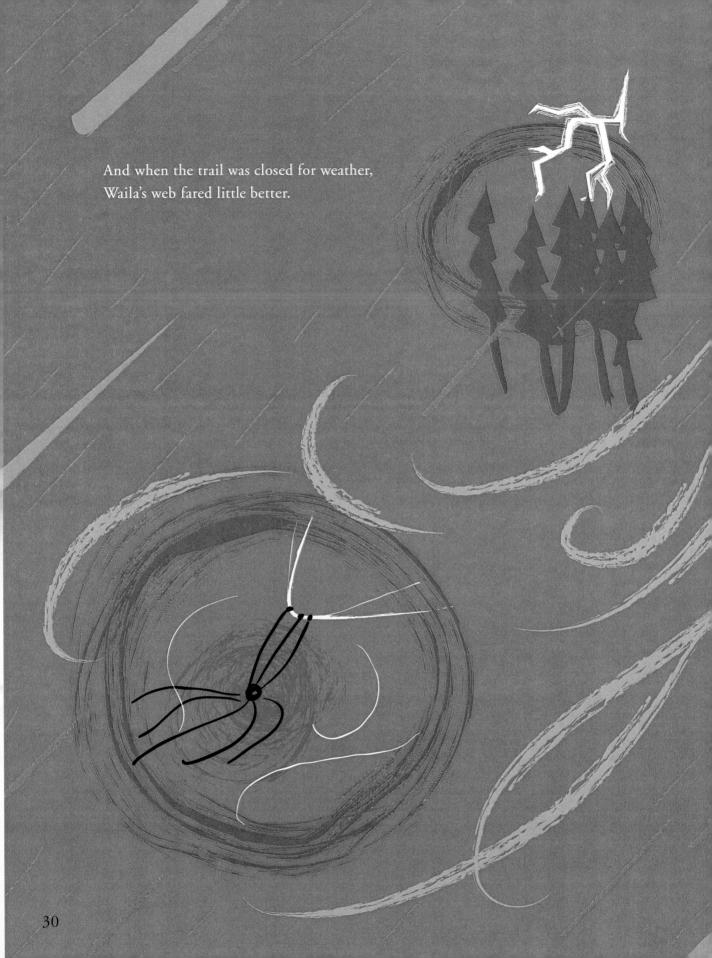

And when the trail was closed for weather,
Waila's web fared little better.

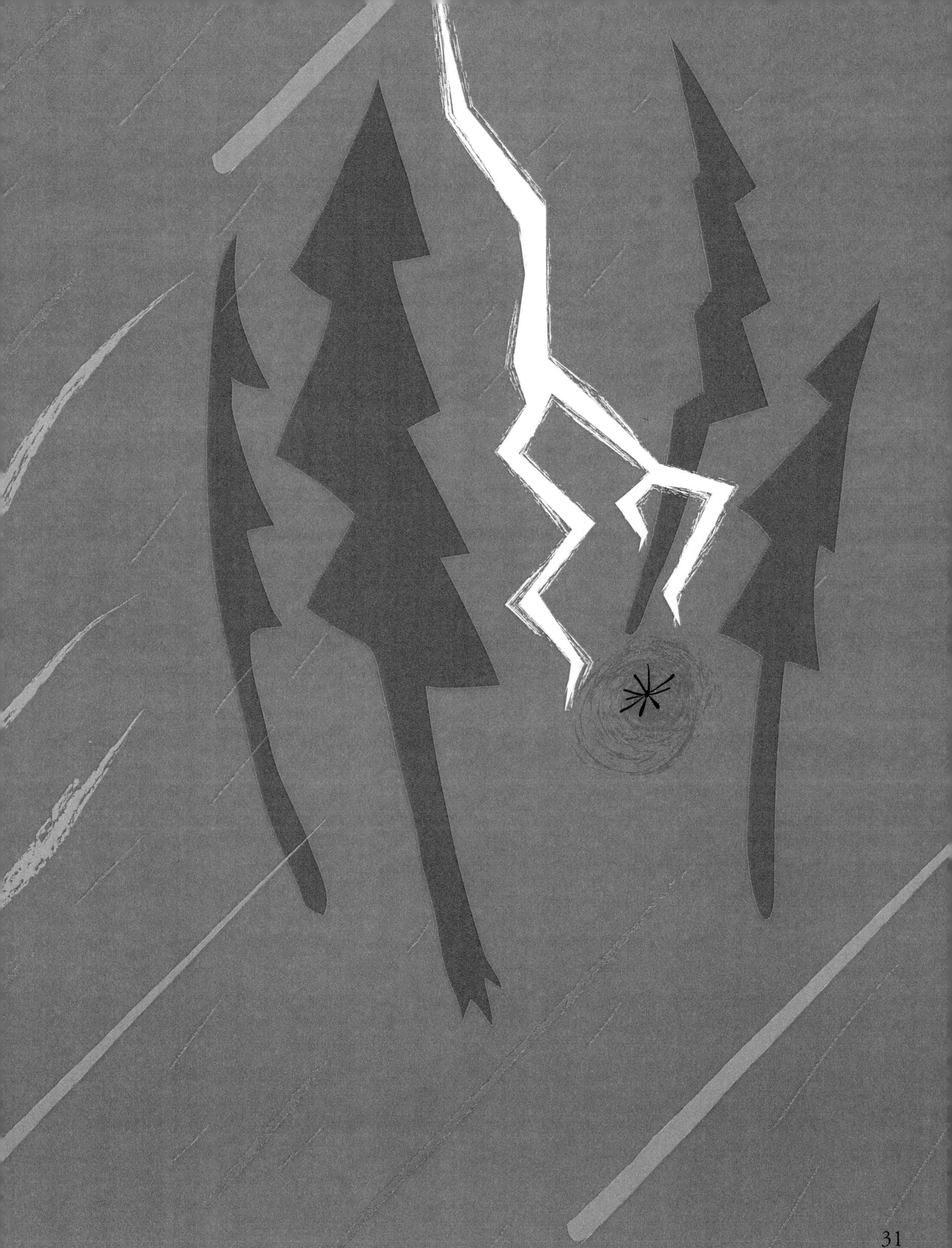

A robin asked a spider,

"What's the point?
Boredom?
Glory?"

The spider said,
"Maybe it's
her head."

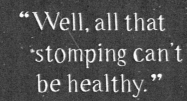

"Well, all that
stomping can't
be healthy."

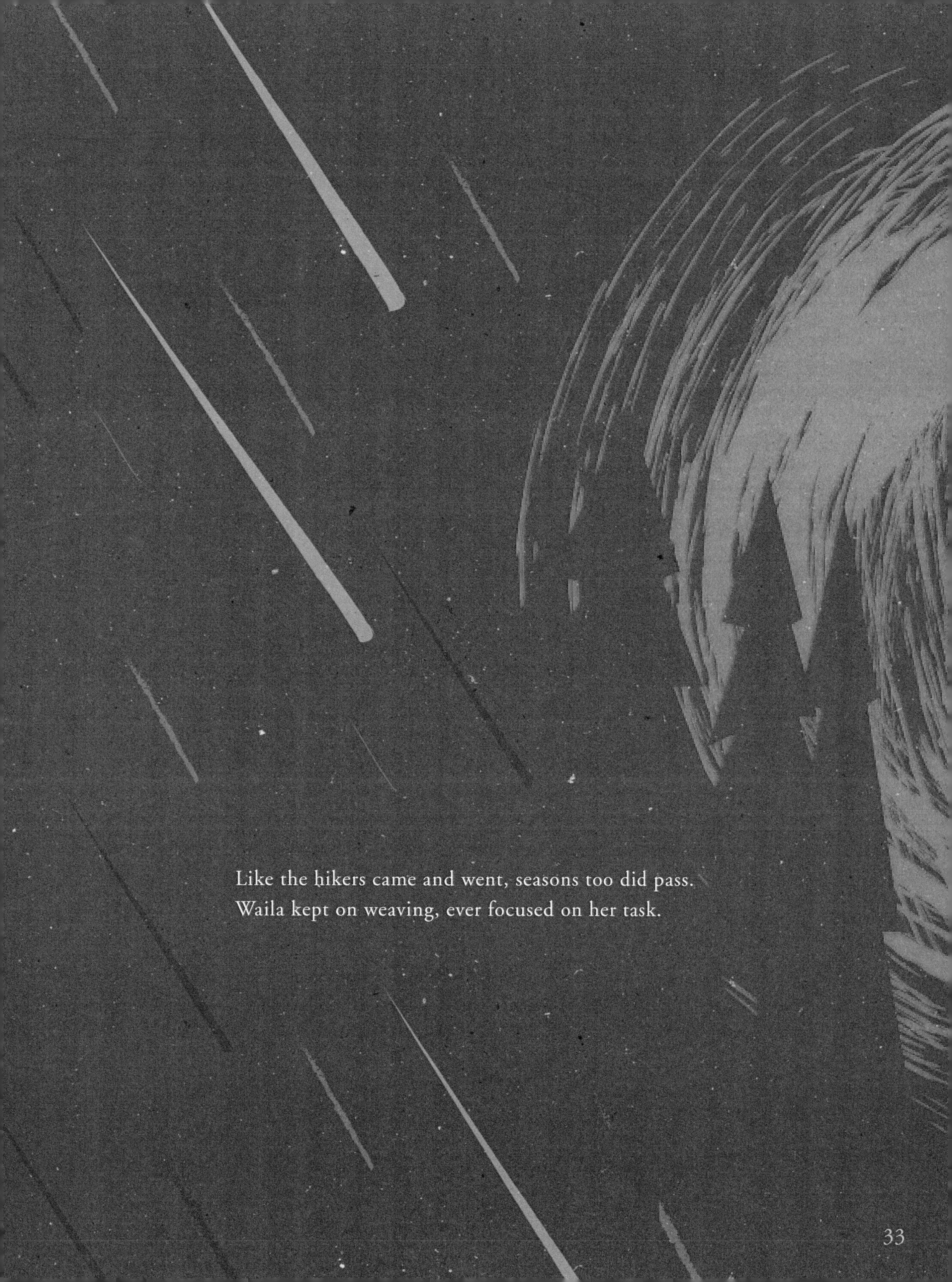

Like the hikers came and went, seasons too did pass.
Waila kept on weaving, ever focused on her task.

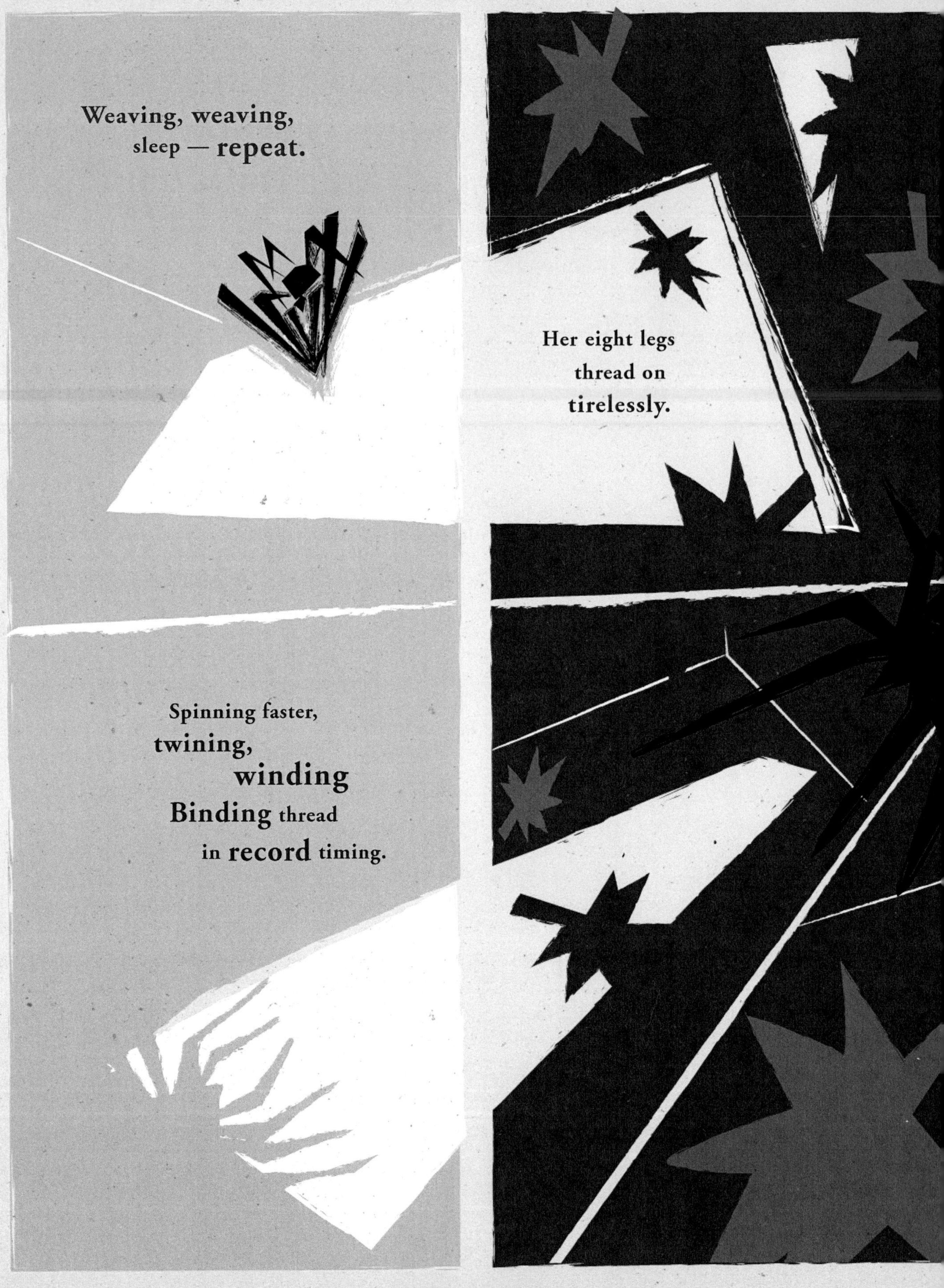
Weaving, weaving,
sleep — repeat.
Her eight legs
thread on
tirelessly.
Spinning faster,
twining,
winding
Binding thread
in record timing.

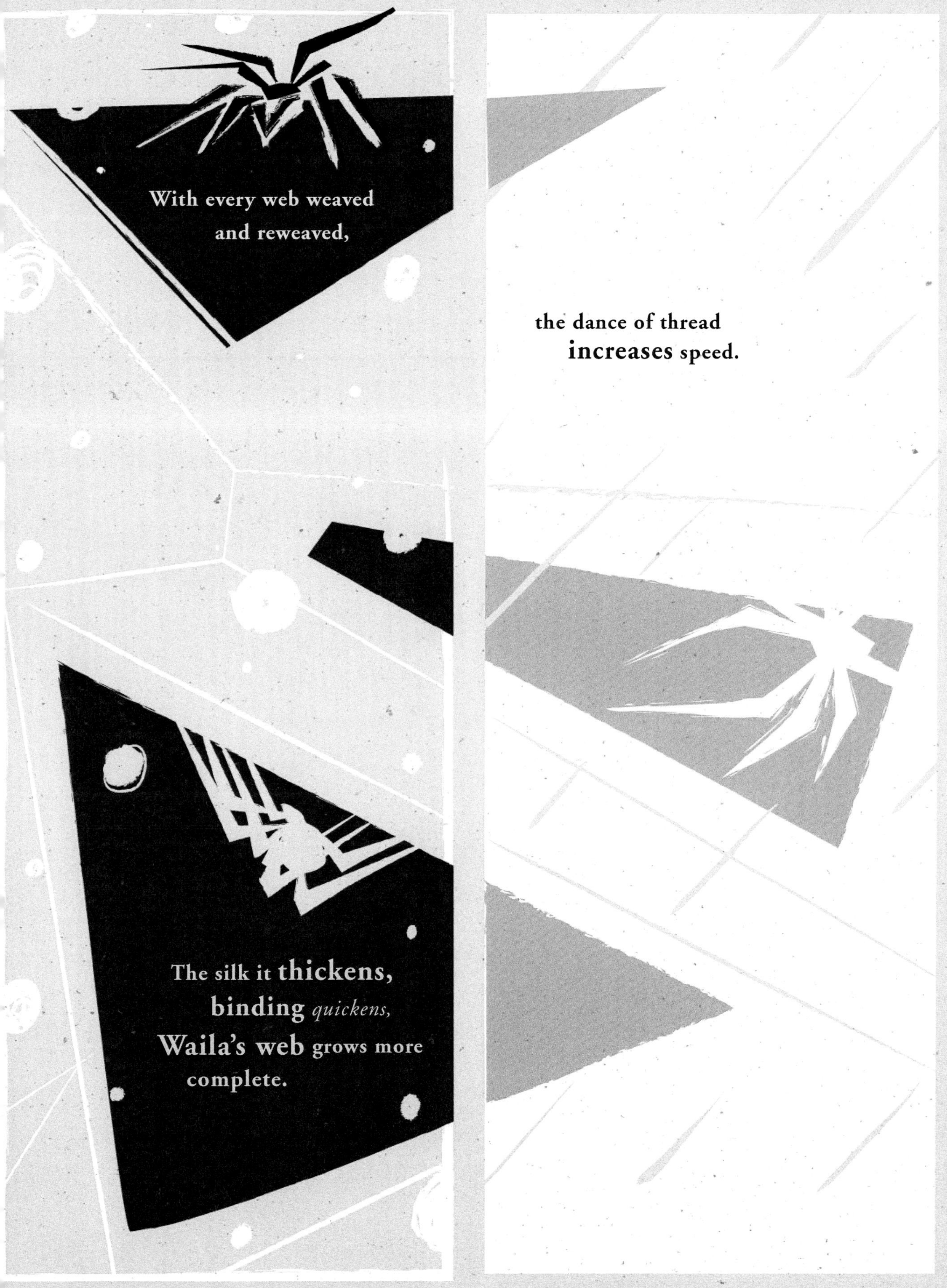

With every web weaved
and reweaved,

the dance of thread
increases speed.

The silk it **thickens**,
binding *quickens*,
Waila's web grows more
complete.

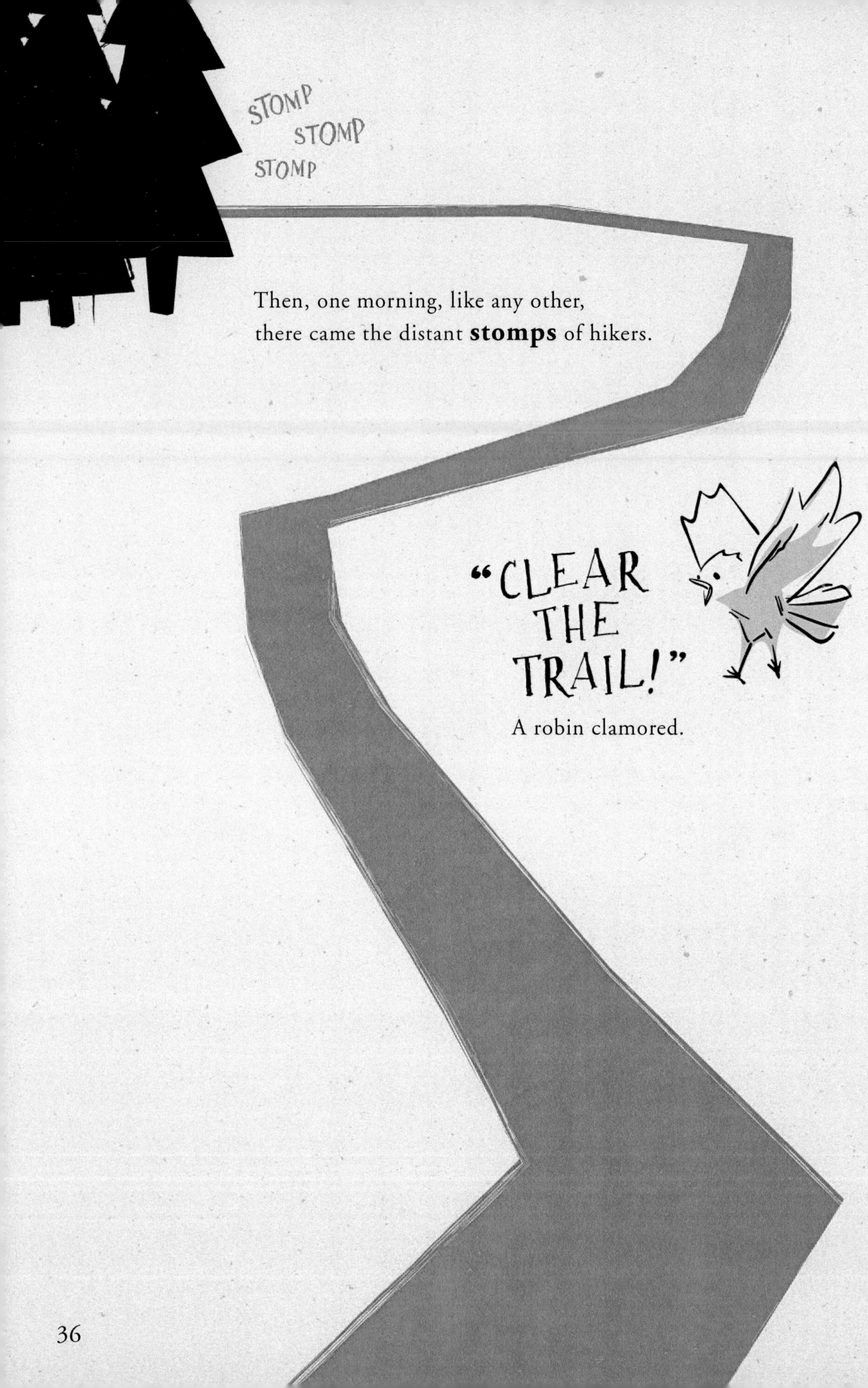
STOMP
STOMP
STOMP
"CLEAR THE TRAIL!"

Then, one morning, like any other,
there came the distant **stomps** of hikers.

A robin clamored.

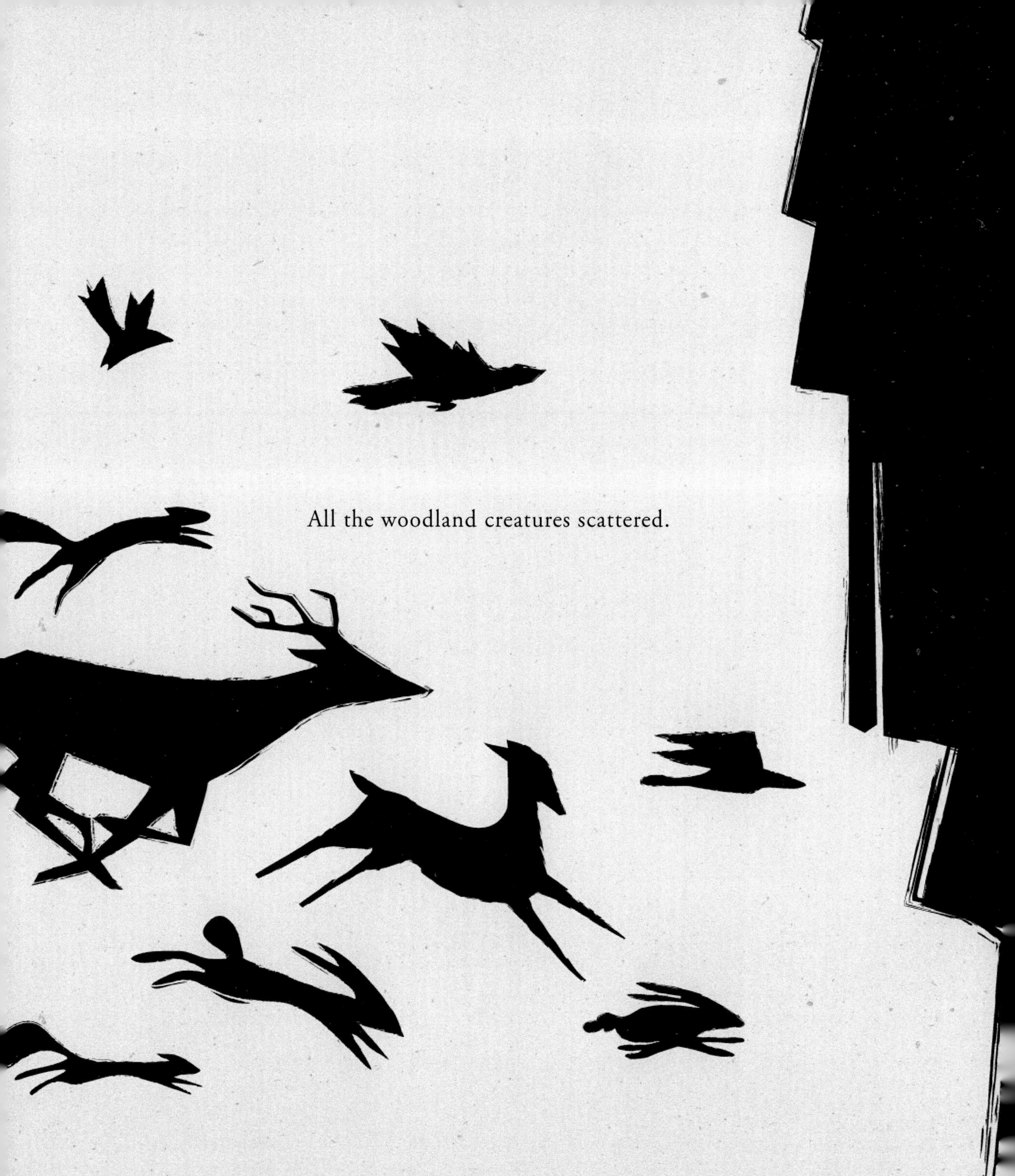

All the woodland creatures scattered.

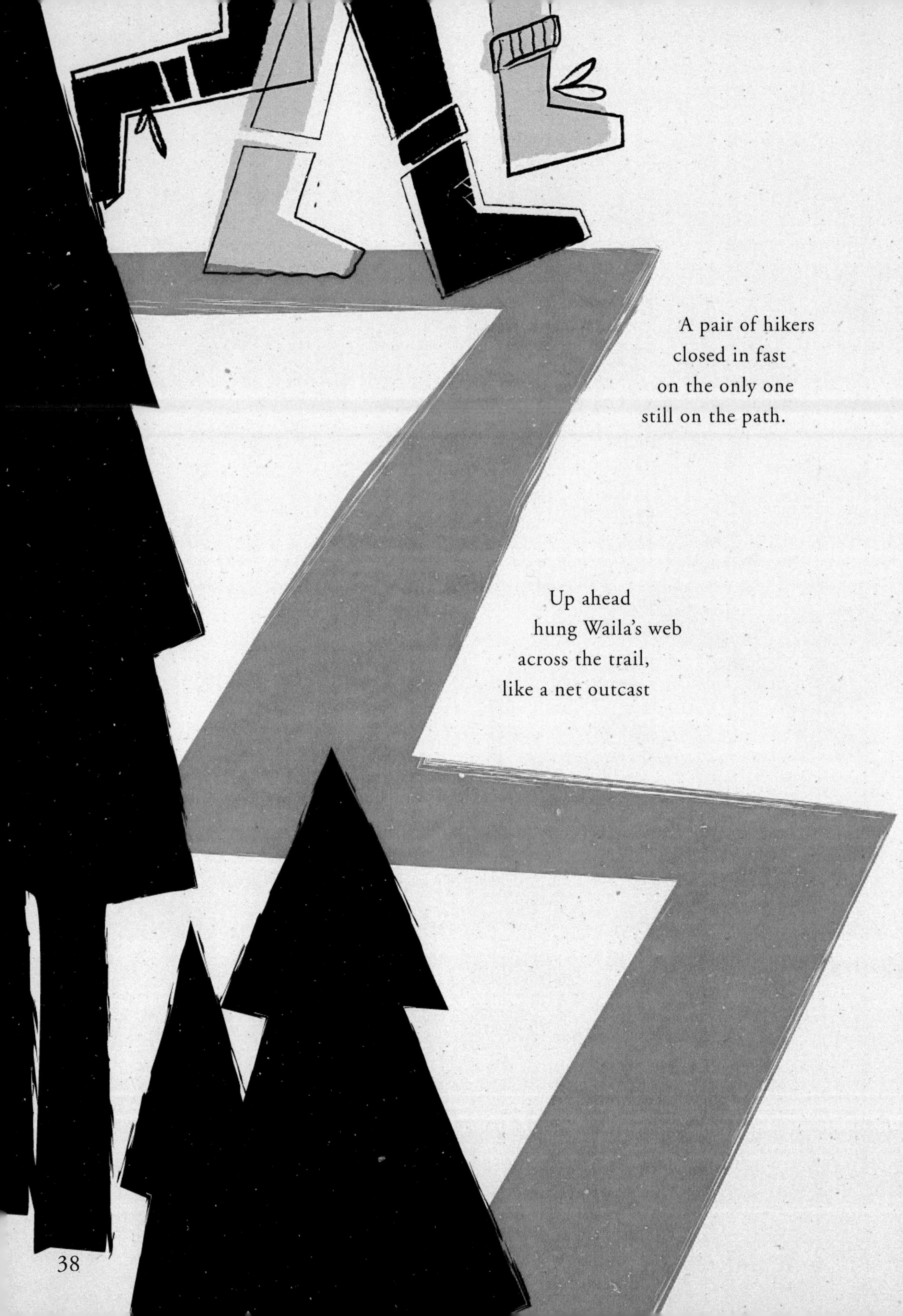

A pair of hikers
closed in fast
on the only one
still on the path.

Up ahead
hung Waila's web
across the trail,
like a net outcast

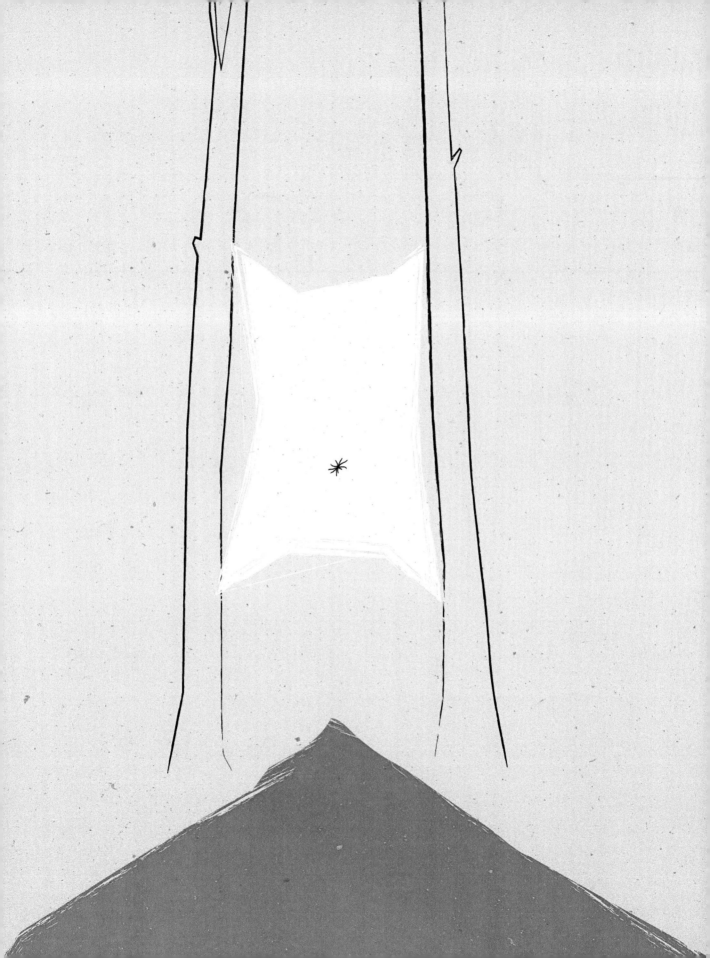

Once again, the spiders tried
to beckon Waila back inside.

"LOOKOUT!" They cried.
"If you don't hide,
It's YOU those boots
will stomp this time!"

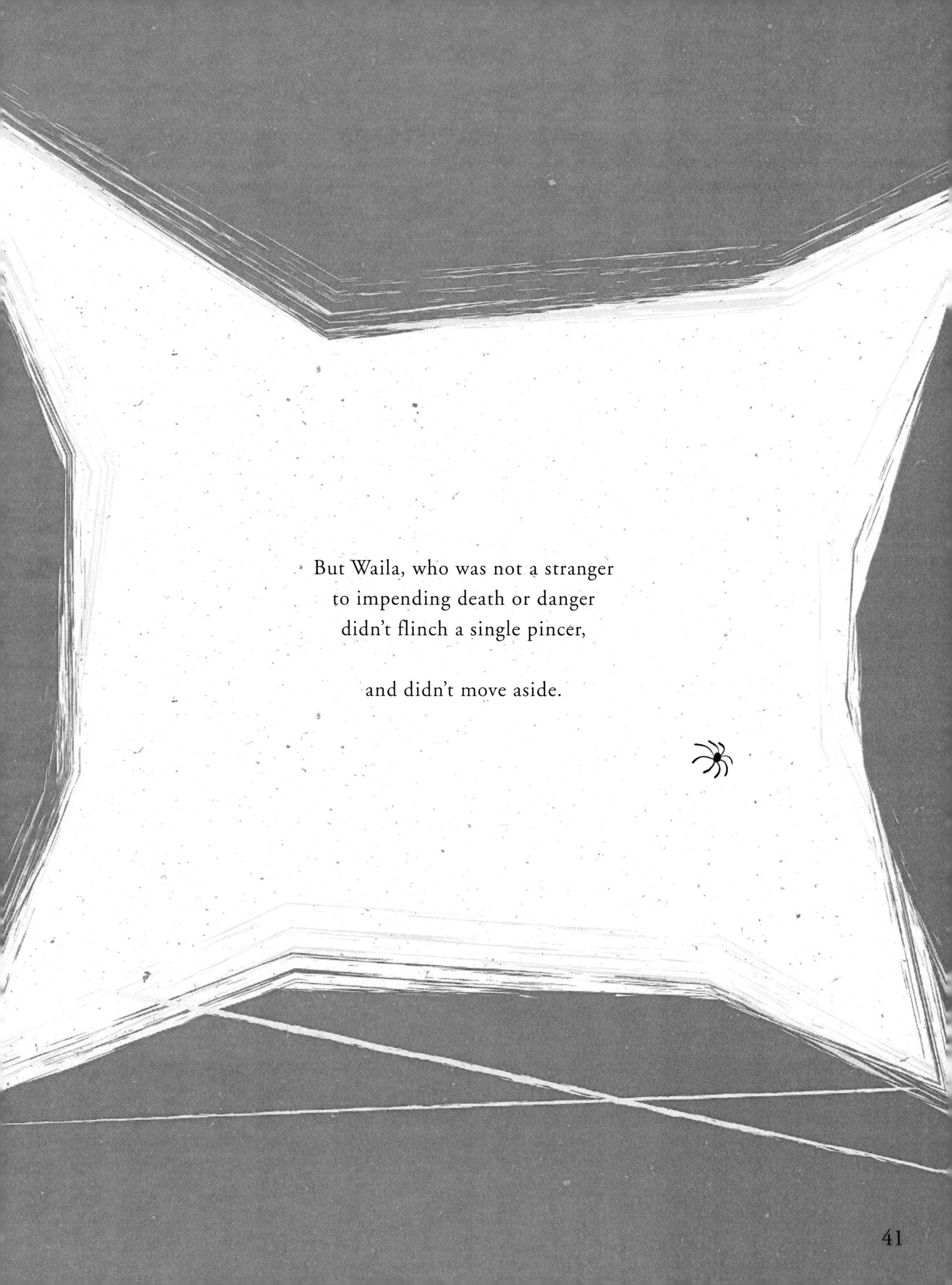

But Waila, who was not a stranger
to impending death or danger
didn't flinch a single pincer,

and didn't move aside.

And so, the hikers came to Waila's web
and would have stomped right through,
But due to Waila's constant weaving,
now her webs had quite improved.

Instead of cutting through the net
of webs with sticks like bayonets,
The men were halted dead mid-stride
by thread, vine-like, from either side!

They pulled and yanked to not avail!
This web was just too strong to fail!

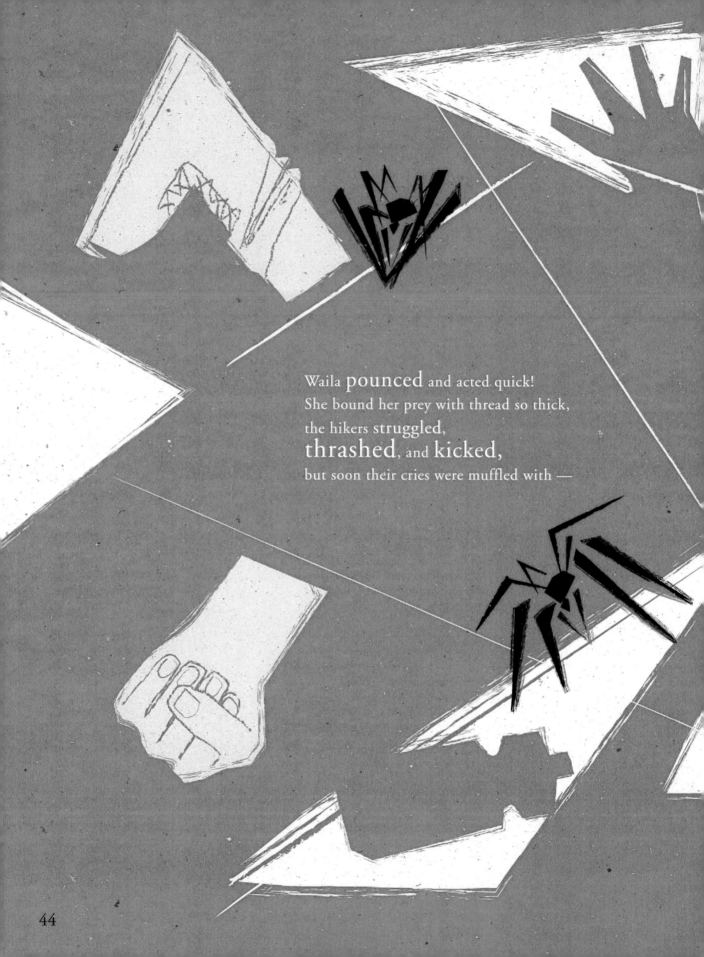

Waila **pounced** and acted quick!
She bound her prey with thread so thick,
the hikers struggled,
thrashed, and **kicked**,
but soon their cries were muffled with —

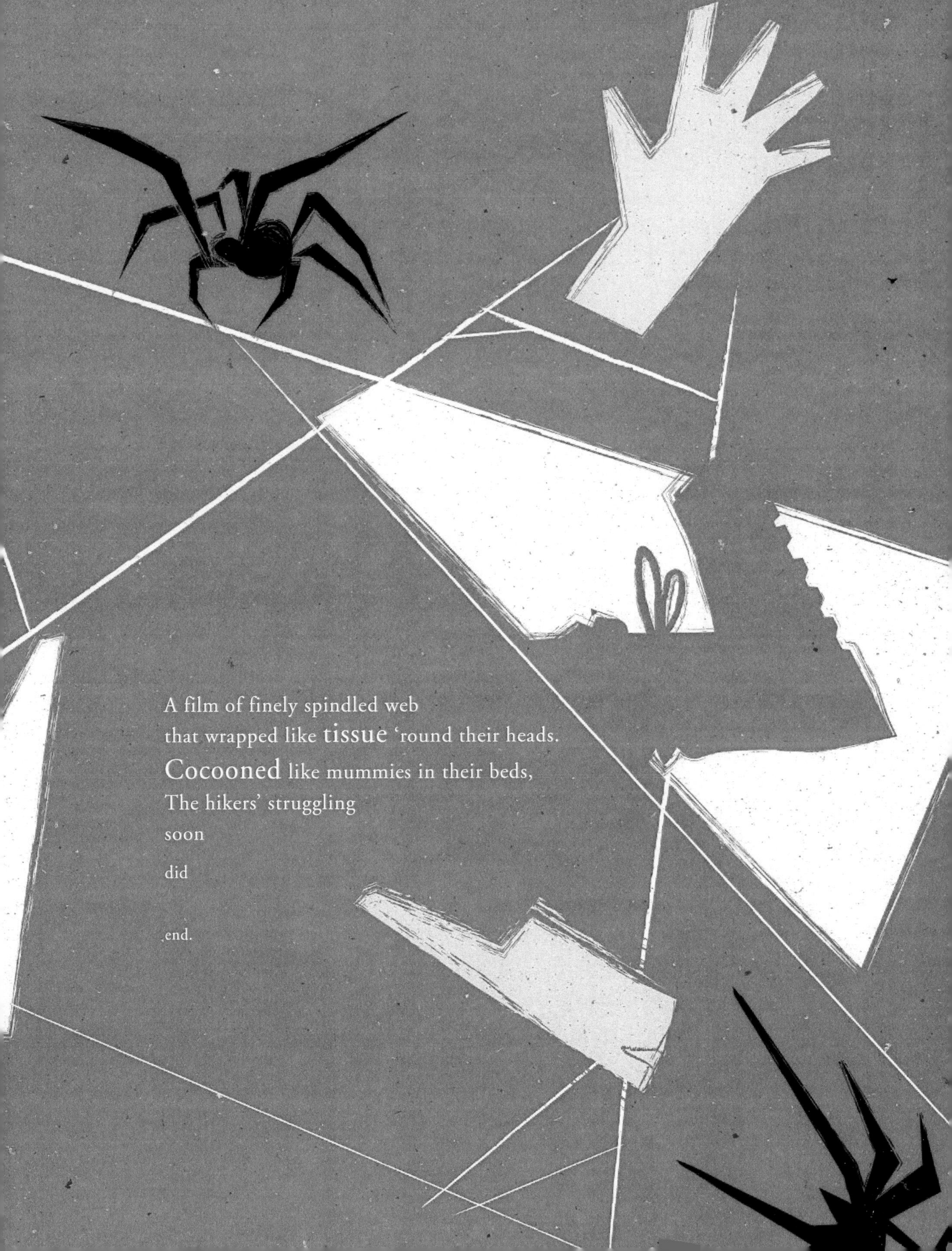

A film of finely spindled web
that wrapped like tissue 'round their heads.
Cocooned like mummies in their beds,
The hikers' struggling
soon
did

end.

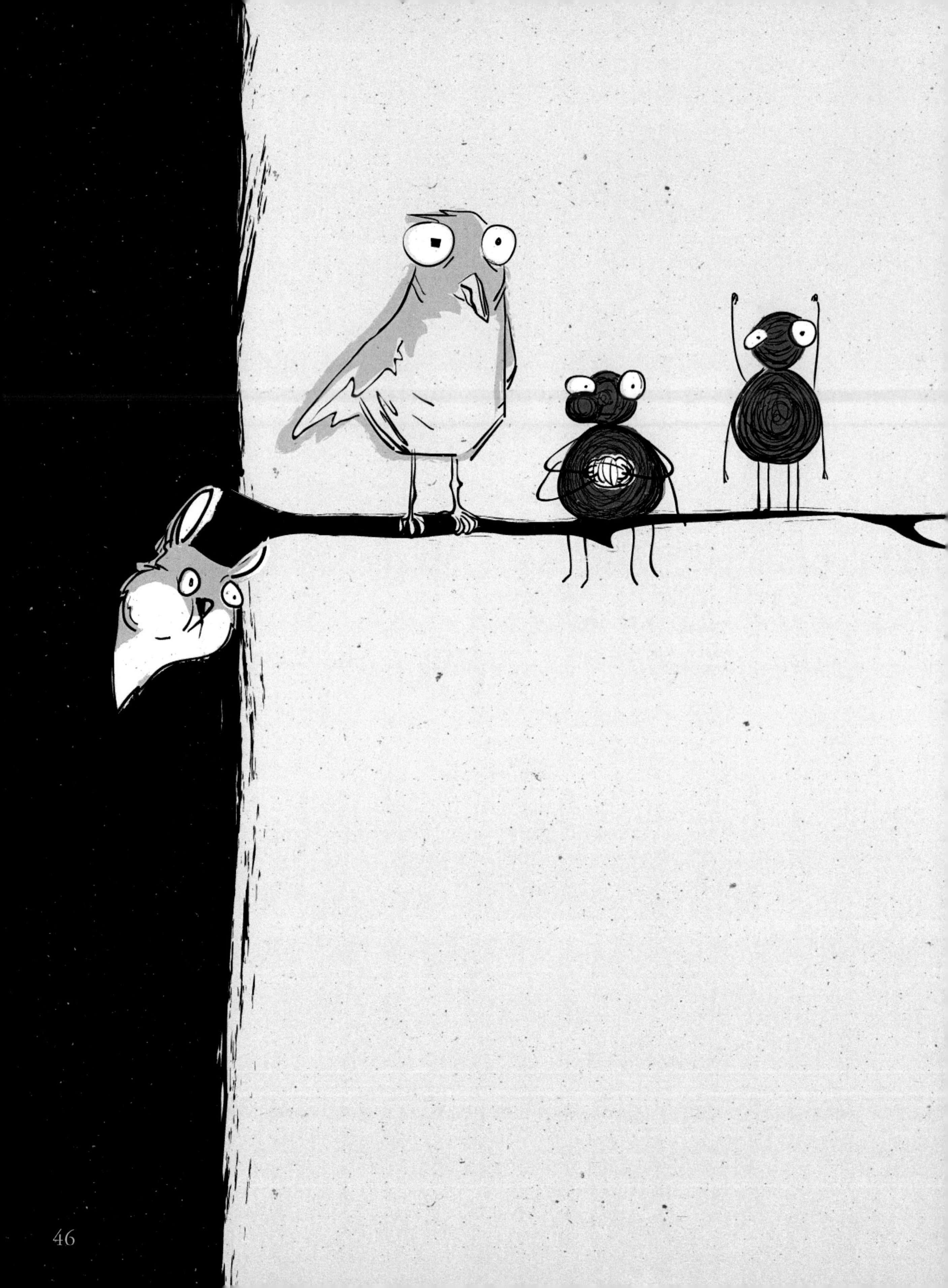

The others looked on, shocked and awed!
All Waila's hard work had paid off!
It seemed she caught a prey so great,
she had food enough to procreate!

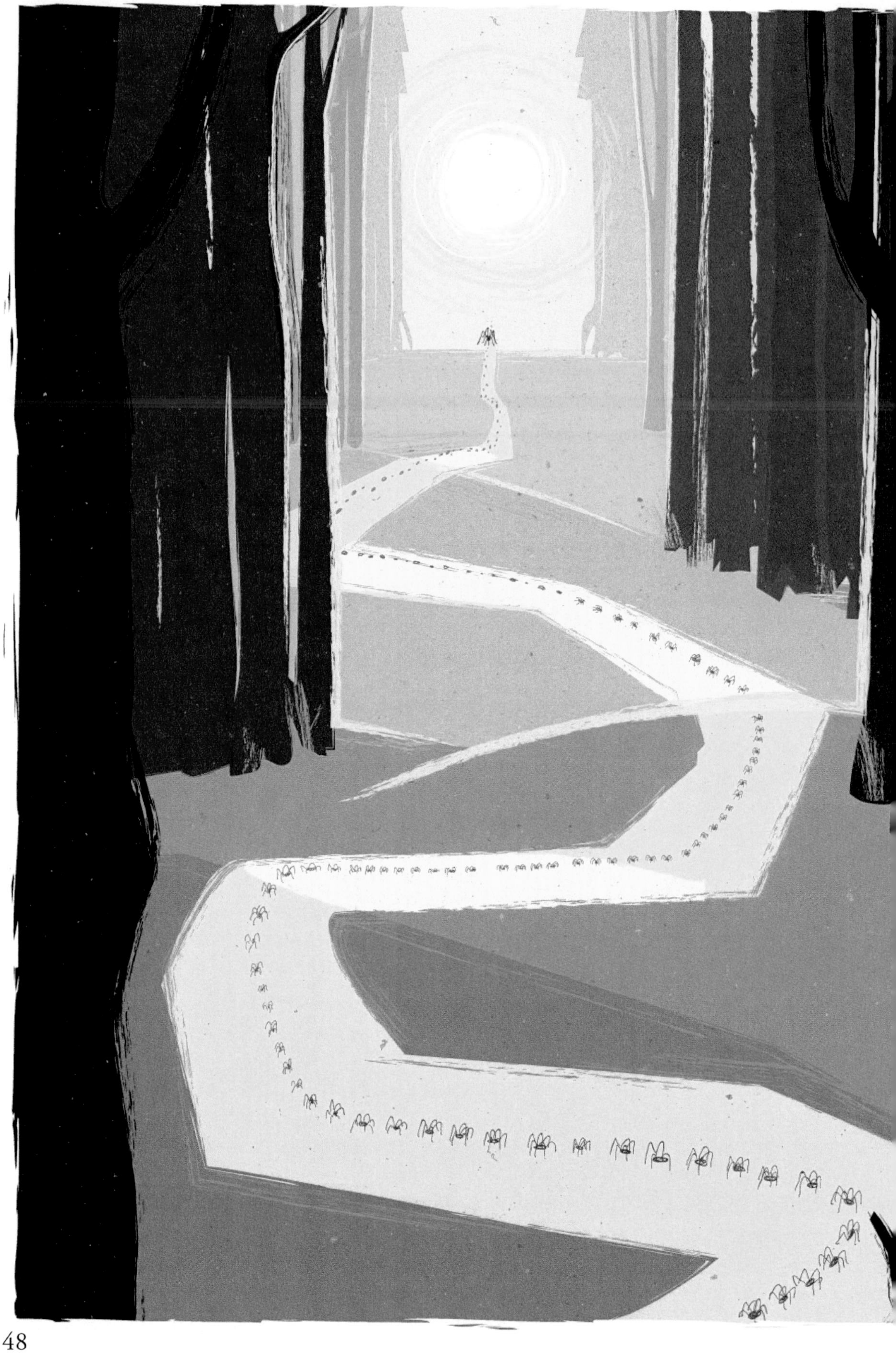

And that's just what good Waila did.
She settled down and had some kids —
400 baby arachnids!
For whom her catch would benefit.

And all her children, and their children,
and their children *never* did
ever have a want or need
to spin or catch a fly again.

So, when you make your masterpiece
and share it with the public,
You'll find they come from far and wide
to **stamp** and **trample** over it.

You'll feel like Waila on the trail,
who failed, and failed,

and failed,

and failed.

You'll want to call it quits and wail,
"ENOUGH! I just can't take it!"

And like a spider spinning in the woods
and out of danger,
you could pick a safer path.
Or *no* path— even safer.

Then you could live on unaware
of what could be if you had dared...

to dream of **bigger things** and spared
a fly...

and caught a hiker.

ABOUT THE AUTHOR

Jessica Paige Dawson graduated from Texas Christian University with a Bachelors of Fine Arts in graphic design. She is an illustrator and Navy Veteran. She lives in Fort Worth, Texas with her husband.

Find out more about this title and other works at JessicaPaigeDawson.com

.

46485055R00035

Made in the USA
San Bernardino, CA
07 August 2019